"Make Me Stop," He Said. "Tell Me This Is Wrong."

Natalie froze. "I can't." She wanted to caress his face, to follow the angles and hard lines, to shape them with her hands. But she couldn't seem to summon the courage.

"Say it," he beckoned.

Silent, she remained where she was, her body flooded with warmth. She needed him, and she couldn't bear to let go, to lose the connection. He closed his eyes. With a quaking hand, she pressed her palm to his chest and felt the erratic beats.

When he opened his eyes, she took her hand away. A minute passed. Or mabe it was a second. For Natalie, time stood still.

"I can't," she said again. "I can't tell you it's wrong."

"Then I'm taking you." Zack's voice turned rough. "I'm taking all of you."

Dear Reader,

Welcome back to another passionate month at Silhouette Desire. A *Scandal Between the Sheets* is breaking out as Brenda Jackson pens the next tale in the scintillating DYNASTIES: THE DANFORTHS series. We all love the melodrama and mayhem that surrounds this Southern family—how about you?

The superb Beverly Barton stops by Silhouette Desire with an extra wonderful title in her bestselling series THE PROTECTORS. *Keeping Baby Secret* will keep *you* on the edge of your seat—and curl your toes all at the same time. What would you do if you had to change your name and your entire history? Sheri WhiteFeather tackles that compelling question when her heroine is forced to enter the witness protection program in *A Kept Woman*. Seems she was a kept woman of another sort, as well...so be sure to pick up this fabulous read if you want the juicy details.

Kristi Gold has written the final, fabulous installment of THE TEXAS CATTLEMAN'S CLUB: THE STOLEN BABY series with *Fit for a Sheikh*. (But don't worry, we promise those sexy cattlemen with be back.) And rounding out the month are two wonderful stories filled with an extra dose of passion: Linda Conrad's dramatic *Slow Dancing With A Texan* and Emilie Rose's supercharged *A Passionate Proposal*.

Enjoy all we have to offer this month—and every month—at Silhouette Desire.

Melissa Jeglinski

Melissa Jeglinski
Senior Editor, Silhouette Desire

Please address questions and book requests to:
Silhouette Reader Service
U.S.: 3010 Walden Ave., P.O. Box 1325, Buffalo, NY 14269
Canadian: P.O. Box 609, Fort Erie, Ont. L2A 5X3

A KEPT WOMAN
SHERI WHITEFEATHER

Silhouette®
Desire

Published by Silhouette Books
America's Publisher of Contemporary Romance

SILHOUETTE BOOKS

ISBN 0-373-76575-4

A KEPT WOMAN

Books by Sheri WhiteFeather

Silhouette Desire

Warrior's Baby #1248
Skyler Hawk: Lone Brave #1272
Jesse Hawk: Brave Father #1278
Cheyenne Dad #1300
Night Wind's Woman #1332
Tycoon Warrior #1364
Cherokee #1376
Comanche Vow #1388
Cherokee Marriage Dare #1478
Sleeping with Her Rival #1496
Cherokee Baby #1509
Cherokee Dad #1523
The Heart of a Stranger #1527
Cherokee Stranger #1563
A Kept Woman #1575

Lone Star Country Club
Lone Wolf

SHERI WHITEFEATHER

lives in Southern California and enjoys ethnic dining, attending powwows and visiting art galleries and vintage clothing stores near the beach. Since her one true passion is writing, she is thrilled to be a part of the Silhouette Desire line. When she isn't writing, she often reads until the wee hours of the morning.

Sheri's husband, a member of the Muscogee Creek Nation, inspires many of her stories. They have a son, a daughter and a trio of cats—domestic and wild. She loves to hear from her readers. You may write to her at: P.O. Box 17146, Anaheim, California 92817. Visit her Web site at www.SheriWhiteFeather.com.

To my readers:
Many of you have commented that you enjoy stories
that push the envelope, and *A Kept Woman*
is no exception. I was particularly fascinated by the
early days of WITSEC (the witness protection program)
and decided to combine some of the early security
methods with the modern program. *A Kept Woman*
is my interpretation of a security field inspector toppling
into a forbidden, heart-bound affair with a witness.
This story blends fact, fiction and creative liberties and
does not necessarily represent the inner workings
of this highly effective and controversial program.

One

Natalie Pascal was nervous. Deputy U.S. Marshal Zack Ryder sensed it from the moment he saw her. As a WITSEC field inspector, he'd encountered plenty of edgy witnesses, and this stunning blonde was no exception. Scanning the passengers filtering into the baggage claim area, he moved forward to make his presence known, to greet the woman he'd been assigned to relocate.

"Natalie." He said her name and she looked up and caught his gaze. For a moment, they just stood in the midst of a bustling airport, staring at each other. Like strangers, he thought, whose lives were about to collide.

"So you're him," she said.

He nodded. "Yep. I'm him. Zack Ryder." Her field

inspector, the deputy marshal who would help Nancy Perris adjust to her new identity, to becoming Natalie Pascal.

She didn't extend her hand and he didn't offer his. He figured she wasn't keen on shaking hands with a lawman, on being too friendly. He'd seen old photographs of her; he knew her history. Prior to her acceptance into the Witness Security Program, she'd been a hot-as-sin, buxom brunette, as well as the girlfriend of a Los Angeles mobster.

These days, she was a reed-thin blonde, with stylishly cropped hair and tinted contacts. The golden-brown color made her eyes seem cougarlike, but he supposed the smoky black liner enhanced the effect, too. Tall and chic, she wore an elegant pantsuit, tailored to fit her slim form.

Zack motioned to the luggage turntable. "Let me know when you see your bags."

She shifted her purse, adjusting the strap on her shoulder. "There's only one."

He didn't comment. He already knew she was traveling light. WITSEC would deliver the rest of her belongings, what little there was. Natalie had liquidated just about everything she owned, everything her mobster boyfriend had given her. "So," he said, reverting to small talk. "How was your flight?"

She glanced away, making him aware of her discomfort. Arriving in an unfamiliar city to meet an unfamiliar man couldn't be easy. But it beat the hell out of the alternative, he thought. Natalie had agreed to testify against her former lover. And if the mob found her, they would kill her. Her old boyfriend wasn't an underling. He was David Halloway, the new boss of the West Coast Family.

Finally, she shifted her gaze back to his, and when she did, they stared at each other again. "My flight was fine. Just fine," she added in a cracked whisper, in a voice so low he could barely hear it.

Because he got the crazy notion to touch her, he broke eye contact. Was she for real? Or was she playing head games? He'd expected her to be a revamped gun moll, but he hadn't predicted the delicate edge of vulnerability.

Zack remained silent. He was pretty good at idle chitchat. But at the moment, communicating with this woman eluded him.

"That one is mine," she said suddenly.

"What?"

She motioned to a suitcase on the turntable. "The one with the gold ribbon."

"Got it." A bit terse, he reached for the bag. Over the years, he'd learned not to trust too deeply, not to allow the criminals-turned-witnesses to con him, not to BS their way into his good graces. He wasn't about to get compromised, especially by a mistress.

He turned to face her, and she took a step back, confusing him even more. "Are you ready?" he asked.

She nodded, and he guided her to the parking lot. It was his job to protect her, to give her a chance to start a new life. And Zack was damn good at his job.

Silent, Natalie walked beside him. Her strides

weren't as long as his, but they were close. She moved like a runway model, like a lean, lithe, sexual creature—a woman who'd gotten by on her looks.

They reached his black sedan and he popped the trunk and stowed her bag. When he opened the passenger door for her, she gave him a hesitant look. Did she think he had a trick up his sleeve because he was behaving like a gentleman?

He climbed behind the wheel, and she buckled her seat belt and gazed out the windshield. He reached for his cigarettes and shook one from the pack. Igniting the tip, he inhaled a gust of nicotine and tobacco, a habit he had no intention of breaking. At forty, he was more than set in his ways.

Squinting through a haze of smoke, Zack backed out of the parking stall, wishing Natalie didn't rub him the wrong way. He'd relocated criminals, as well as innocent people. Husbands, wives, children. Families who'd sacrificed their safety to do the right thing. He wasn't sure where Natalie Pascal fit in. For the first time in his career, a witness had managed to baffle him.

He slid her a sideways glance, and she pushed her bangs out of her eyes. "Are you all right?" he asked.

She placed her hands on her lap. "Why wouldn't I be?"

"This is a monumental change. Different from what you're used to."

"I can handle it."

Could she? he wondered. She'd been a kept woman for most of her adult life and, at twenty-nine, that left her out of the mainstream loop. "It's okay to be scared."

She barely blinked. "Scared? About relocating to Idaho? I'm looking forward to living in Coeur d'Alene. I've heard it's a nice place."

"Yes, it is." But he wasn't buying her I'm-in-control facade. Although WITSEC had provided her with psychological counseling to prepare her for the move, she was still anxious, he thought. Restless about her future, afraid the West Coast Family would find her.

"WITSEC showed me a videotape of Coeur d'Alene," she said.

"I know," he responded, wondering why she'd agreed to testify against her former lover. Revenge? Fear? With Natalie, he couldn't be sure.

What kind of woman would sleep with a mobster? A married mobster, no less. Her affair with David Halloway shouldn't matter, but the idea twisted Zack's gut, reminding him of the day he'd caught his ex-wife in bed with another man.

When his knuckles whitened on the steering wheel, he eased his grip. In a roundabout way, his wife had blamed him for her infidelity, claiming his job had interfered with their marriage. But that was a load of bull. In Zack's mind, cheating was cheating. He wasn't about to take responsibility for something that wasn't his fault.

Natalie stared straight ahead, watching the bumper of the car in front of them. For the past thirty minutes, the ride had been quiet, the conversation stilted.

Why did Zack Ryder have to remind her of David? They didn't look anything alike, but the deputy marshal was big and tough and brimming with power. He possessed a domineering presence, just like David. The man she'd loved. The man who'd destroyed her.

She shifted in her seat, then turned to study Zack's profile. His neatly trimmed hair was a deep, dark shade of brown, and his temples and sideburns bore faint threads of gray. He was handsome, in a hard, imposing sort of way. She knew WITSEC inspectors were highly trained security specialists, but Zack made her nervous. Then again, this whole experience made her nervous.

The trial was still a ways off, but the Marshal Service had promised to provide around-the-clock protection when she returned to L.A. to testify. Of course, this was different. Zack wouldn't be with her twenty-four hours a day. Natalie wasn't in a "danger area." She was on highway 90, heading for Coeur d'Alene.

WITSEC had gone to great lengths to establish her new identity, to alter her appearance, to help Nancy Perris disappear. They'd kept her in a secure location until they felt it was safe to put her on a plane and send her to Idaho. To meet Zack Ryder.

He glanced over at her and for one pulse-jarring second, she froze. When he turned back to the road, she let out the breath she'd been holding.

In spite of the help she'd been getting from the Marshal Service, Natalie wasn't comfortable around lawmen. The good-cop bad-cop thing set her on edge. She could never tell who was who.

"We're almost there," Zack said.

"We are?" She opened her purse, prepared to reapply her lipstick, then realized what she was doing. Fumbling with her bag, she cursed her stupidity. David had encouraged her to primp, to make sure she looked perfect every time she appeared in public. It was a habit she couldn't seem to break. Her fingers itched to secure her compact, but she closed her purse instead. She wasn't about to flip open her mirror and gloss up her lips in front of Zack.

"Are you hungry?" he asked.

Still stressing over her compact, she looked up. "What?"

"Do you want to eat?"

She shook her head. Food was the furthest thing from her mind.

He gave her a quick study. "I'll bet you refused the meal on your plane, too."

Natalie didn't respond. She'd been told that her field inspector would play a definitive role in her relocation, that his commitment to her would be on a long-term basis. Yet she couldn't imagine sharing her emotions with this man. She wasn't about to admit that she'd awakened this morning, fresh from a nightmare and battling a stomachache.

He exited the highway and headed into town. Curious, she peered out the window. The sidewalks of Coeur d'Alene were busy, the shops quaint and inviting. She liked the idea of living in a resort community, but her quest for independence wasn't nearly as liberating as she'd hoped it would be. The newness made her feel like a knobby-kneed kid on the first day of school.

As Zack turned onto another street and pulled into a parking lot, she noticed the sandwich shop. "What are you doing?" she asked.

"Getting us some lunch."

"Us?"

"Yes, us. We're both going to eat. I'm not going to let you waste away. Not on my watch."

Because his concern seemed genuine, she fought a wave of confusion. He was big and strong, and a part of her wanted to cling to him. But she'd made that mistake with David. No matter how lonely she was, no matter how much she longed for a friend, she wouldn't allow herself to need another man. Not even her field inspector.

"You don't have to fuss over me," she told him.

"Good grief, woman. It's just a sandwich."

No, she thought. It was more than that. So much more.

Zack got out of the car, leaving her alone with her thoughts. He disappeared into the eatery, and she recalled the first meal David had bought her. She'd been a love-starved teenager living on the streets, seduced by the comfort of one simple lunch.

Zack returned a short while later. He put the sodas he'd purchased in the cup holder between their seats and handed her the bag. "You can have your pick. Ham and cheese or roast beef and avocado."

When their gazes locked, she realized her stomachache was gone. In its place was a warm little flutter. God help her, she thought. She was attracted to him.

Stunned by the sexual pull, she glanced at his left hand. She didn't see a ring, but that didn't mean anything. David hadn't worn a ring, either. In the beginning, she hadn't known her lover was married.

"Ham and cheese is fine," she said, guilt clouding her mind. She'd left David when she'd learned the truth, but it hadn't taken long for him to convince her to return to him, to be his mistress. And that shamed her most of all.

Zack started the car, and she realized he was taking her to her new home. She'd been told that he would rent her a place, a temporary dwelling until she could find a house of her own.

Natalie kept the sandwich bag on her lap, crinkling a corner of the paper. The rustling sound was better than silence, she decided. Better than the strange energy between her and Zack.

He headed toward the lake, and she rolled down the window to breathe in a gust of fresh air. She could see a glimpse of the water, sparkling in the distance. A body of blue, she thought. As tranquil as a tourist's dream, as active as a child's imagination.

Her view of the lake disappeared when he turned onto a tree-lined street. Natalie had never lived in an area like this. She'd been welfare poor; she'd been mistress rich. But she'd never fit into the white-picket-fence world.

He guided the car down a long driveway and stopped at a cozy guest house. Her heart bumped her chest. The windows were trimmed in yellow and the lawn was freshly mowed.

"Is this mine? I expected an apartment."

He parked his sedan and cut the engine. "It rents by the month, so it didn't require a lease. The owners live up front. They're a young family. They seem like nice folks."

"What did you tell them about me?"

"That you're a friend of mine who plans to open a boutique in Coeur d'Alene."

That was close to the truth, she thought. Except for the friend part. "Did you mention that you're a deputy?"

"Yes, but no one outside the Marshal Service knows I'm with WITSEC. As far as your landlords are concerned, I'm just a local deputy."

Natalie fell silent. It was obvious his badge had closed the deal. Who wouldn't trust a federal lawman?

When he exited the car, she followed suit, carrying the sandwich bag. He turned to look at her, and when that little flutter returned to her stomach, she struggled to temper it.

The June air was warm, and a mild breeze blew. Zack stood tall and dark in a black jacket and matching trousers. The sun had bronzed his skin and his eyes were marked with tiny lines. Frown lines, she thought. He shifted their sodas, then handed her one, searching his pockets for the keys to her new home. She wondered if he'd been raised in this area. Maybe he was a member of the Coeur d'Alene Indian tribe. Zack looked as if he might be part Native American.

Finally, he located the keys and unlocked the front door. She stepped inside and tried to contain her excitement. The living room presented a stone hearth, and the kitchen had French doors that led to a barbecue deck. Already she loved it.

"There isn't much here by the way of furnishings," he said. "I got you a bed and a dresser. And a dining room table. Just a few things to help you get by. You can pick out whatever else you need."

"Thank you." When their eyes met, an indefinable moment passed between them. Heat? Hunger? A stream of tenderness? Natalie couldn't tell.

"But just remember that you're on a budget," he added. "WITSEC will foot the bill for your furniture, but they aren't going to provide the fancy-ass stuff Halloway used to buy for you."

She tried not to flinch. "Excuse me?"

"Excuse you for what? Being spoiled? Don't worry, you'll get over it."

Natalie's heart fell. Yes, she had slept with a married man. And yes, she was guilty, shamed to the bone. But wasn't it enough that David's wife vowed to see her dead? Did she have to be judged by a U.S. marshal, as well? Summoning the strength to defy him, she held his gaze. "At least I have enough money to start a business."

"By selling off everything lover-boy gave you? That's not the same as earning it."

She held her ground. "I'm sure it's more than you have."

He didn't back down. "I've made some investments."

She pushed the issue. "I probably still have more than you."

"Maybe, but I'm not a hot-looking blonde." He shrugged, then made a silly joke, turning the tide with his offbeat humor. "Can you imagine some mobster putting me up in a condo? Dressing me in sexy lingerie?"

She rolled her eyes, and he laughed.

"You're a jerk, Deputy. And you're not funny."

He grinned at her. "Then how come you're fighting a smile?"

Because I'm an idiot, she thought. And she'd been charmed by jerks before. Refusing to break down and smile, she grabbed her drink and sucked on the straw.

"So what do you think of this place?" he asked.

Feigning indifference, she swallowed the soda. "It's okay."

"Just okay? I thought it was perfect for a single woman. It even has one of those glamour bathrooms. Big sunken tub, lights around the mirror." He took the sandwiches from her and placed them on the dining room table. "Come on, I'll show you around."

She accepted the tour, but she kept her distance, making sure their hands didn't accidentally touch or their shoulders didn't brush when she squeezed past him in the hallway.

The curtains in the bedroom matched the carpet, and the brass bed he'd provided was made up with a fluffy white quilt and lacy pillows. She shot him a curious glance.

He defended his choice. "What the hell do I know? It seemed like something a woman would like. Besides, it was on sale."

She thought the bed was pretty, but she wasn't about to admit it. "Where do you live?" she asked, wondering what sort of furnishings he favored.

"I commute between a cabin in the mountains and a house in the city."

But he wasn't going to tell her what mountain range or what city, she realized. He knew everything about her, but she wasn't privy to personal information about him.

"You have my pager number, don't you?" he asked suddenly.

Natalie nodded. WITSEC had provided it.

"It's a satellite pager," he said. "I won't miss your calls." He moved toward the dresser, where a telephone sat. "I left a list of local numbers, too. Fire, police. But if you think you're in danger, call the one at the top. That'll bring a squad of marshals to your door."

Her pulse jumped to her throat. She hoped and prayed that she would never have to use that number, but she knew the possibility existed.

As Zack continued the tour, she followed, trying to keep her fear in check. In a fit of anger, David had killed one of his associates, then forced her to help him clean up the mess. The blood, the—

"Check out the bathroom."

She blinked. "What?"

"The bathroom."

She peered around his shoulder, and he moved out of the way. The tile-lined tub, she noticed, was big enough for two, and a floral-print curtain shielded a separate shower stall.

Speaking of flowers. An artistic bouquet decorated the sink. Pink, purple and red blooms flourished in an elegant glass vase. "Are these from my landlords?"

"No."

"Then who ordered them?"

"I did."

Stunned, she merely stared at him. "You?" The man who'd criticized her character? "Are flowers a standard WITSEC procedure?"

"No, but I thought they would brighten up the place."

"Thank you." Up until now, she'd been living in a safe-site center, where the doors were electronically bolted and hallways were monitored with security cameras and motion detectors. It hadn't felt like home.

He finished showing her around and suggested they eat lunch. She sat across from him at the table, confused by his ever changing moods. He seemed judgmental one minute and compassionate the next.

He unwrapped the roast beef sandwich. "I made sure the kitchen was pretty well stocked. Dishes, pots, pans, silverware." He motioned behind him. "The fridge came with the place. We can go to the market later if you want."

She picked the onions out of her sandwich. "We?"

"You don't have a car yet. Who else is supposed to take you shopping?"

Who indeed? Zack Ryder was her only contact in Coeur d'Alene. But that didn't mean she had to make herself vulnerable to him, she thought. So he'd bought her flowers. So what? It was his job to help witnesses adjust to their new surroundings.

"When can I meet my landlords?" she asked.

"Next week. They're on vacation right now."

"What are their names?"

"Steve and Carla. He's an accountant, and she runs after the kids. A couple of towheaded boys." Zack chuckled. "From what I gathered, they keep her pretty busy."

Already Natalie felt a pang of envy. All of her life she'd wanted to be a loving wife and a good, caring mother. But instead, she'd become a toy, a blow-up doll for her lover's amusement. "I used to be a brunette."

He gave her a perplexed look. "I'm aware of that, but what does your old hair color have to do with your new landlords?"

"Nothing. You called me a hot-looking blonde earlier. But I was a brunette when I was with David."

"I wasn't making a literal statement. And you're beautiful either way."

"I don't need you to compliment me."

He frowned at her. "I'm not stroking your ego. I'm just stating the facts. You're going to get a lot of attention no matter where you live. You're going to turn some heads."

Was she supposed to downplay her appearance? She'd tried to create a classy image, to mold herself into someone new. "Does that bother you?"

"Why would it?" he responded a bit too defensively.

"No reason." She tasted her food and battled the annoying little flutter in her stomach. The telltale sign that she was attracted to her field inspector, a man who made her much too aware of her past as another man's mistress.

Two

Zack didn't like the sexual vibe that stretched between him and Natalie. He wanted to blame her for it, to tell her to knock it off, but how could he? All she was doing was sitting across from him, rejecting the onions in her sandwich.

But somehow she still managed to stir his imagination. Then again, he'd heard all sorts of things about her. Hot, erotic things. Mob rumors, he supposed. Stories the FBI had passed on to the Marshal Service. Not that Zack normally lent an ear to gossip, but he'd been weaned on organized crime. His uncle had worked for the Marshal Service when the LCN—La Cosa Nostra—had been riding high. And although the West Coast Family wasn't part of the Italian Mafia, they'd patterned their organization after the guys his uncle used to tell him about.

Zack couldn't remember who'd circulated the rumors about Natalie. It wasn't Uncle Joe. He died before the West Coast Family had come into power. But either way, Zack recalled hearing about Nancy Perris. And now here he was, helping her relocate.

According to legend, Nancy was every mobster's dream. She was good with her hands and even better with her mouth. She got off on arousing David Halloway in public places, in putting her head in his lap.

Was any of that true? Zack didn't know, but like the red-blooded, sexually obsessed male he was, he had weird fantasies about finding out, about straight-out asking her.

"Is your sandwich okay?" he asked instead.

She nodded and reached for her napkin.

He watched her wipe a drop of mayonnaise from her lips, and while she dabbed at the creamy condiment, his groin sent a dangerous signal to his brain. He nearly cursed out loud. The last thing he needed was to fall under her do-you-want-me-to-put-my-head-in-your-lap? spell. He couldn't remember the last time a woman had done that to him.

"Is yours?" she said.

He shifted in his chair. "Is my what?"

"Sandwich good?"

"I get these pretty often." He picked up his drink and tried to douse the unwelcome desire. If Zack had a lover, he would go straight home and get laid.

Natalie looked up. "How much time am I going to have to spend with you?"

Too much, he thought. "That depends on how long it takes to get you settled." For the first month, he normally dealt with a relocated family on a daily, Monday through Friday basis, but he never really knew what to expect. Some witnesses required more guidance than others. "We need to work out a schedule so I can familiarize you with the area, find you a car, help you scout locations for your boutique." Pausing, he glanced around. "And finish furnishing this house."

"I want to enroll in school, too."

"Of course." He knew she had plans to further her education. All she had was a high-school diploma to her name—her old name and her new one. WITSEC only supplied documents to which a witness was entitled.

"I was told North Idaho College has workforce-training classes."

Curious, he sat back, gauging her. "What are you interested in taking?"

"Business-related courses."

Could she be a little more specific? "To prepare you for the boutique?"

She squared her shoulders. "Yes, but I worked at a clothing store. I have experience to rely on, too."

Her confident posture didn't fool him. From what he understood, her job as a salesclerk had been short-lived, a few months at best. "That was a long time ago."

"It'll come back to me."

"I'm sure school will help." According to Natalie's file, she'd met David Halloway at one of his strip clubs, auditioning to be a lap dancer. And that, he thought, was a far cry from a retail store. "I'll drive you to the college tomorrow. You can pick up a catalog."

"What about my furniture? Can we take care of that tomorrow, as well?"

"Sure."

She blew out an audible breath. "I need to increase my wardrobe, too. My old clothes don't fit anymore. WITSEC got me some new things, but the selection is rather limited."

Zack studied the top of her pantsuit. "Looks like you finagled some nice duds to me."

"Finagled?" Her eyes, those smoky cat eyes, turned sharp. "I've gone from a size twelve to a size eight within a matter of months. What was I supposed to wear on this trip? A gunnysack? Or did you expect WITSEC to send me to Idaho naked?"

He cleared his throat. Picturing her naked wasn't on the agenda. "Fine. I'll take you to the mall when I get a chance. But don't ask me to arrange for the funds. That wasn't part of your MOU."

"Don't preach to me about my Memorandum of Understanding. I'm well aware of what was in it." Defiant, she lifted her chin. "I'm more than capable of buying my own clothes."

And living on the stipend WITSEC provided, he

thought. Until she got her business off the ground, the government would be paying her way.

Finally, they finished their lunch. She crumpled their trash and stuffed it back into the bag. Before things turned tense again, he asked, "Do you want to get groceries now?"

She shook her head. "Truthfully? I don't feel like going back out."

"Then give me a list and I'll take care of it." He wasn't about to leave her with an empty fridge. She already looked as though she starved herself.

"That sounds fine to me." She rose to get her purse, which she'd left on the kitchen counter.

He turned to watch her, to wonder what her audition as a lap dancer had been like. Had she gotten the job? Zack couldn't be sure. There were no tax records linking her to Halloway's clubs, but that didn't mean she and Halloway hadn't cheated Uncle Sam, keeping Natalie's earnings off the books.

She returned with a pen and paper and a tiny spiral-bound notebook she must have had in her bag. While she concentrated on a grocery list, he tried to evaluate her. Some of Halloway's strippers turned tricks, but Natalie had snared the boss.

She handed over the paper, and he scanned the items she'd requested. She'd kept it simple, but she seemed more interested in buying clothes than food. Or taking off her clothes, he reminded himself. Halloway's clubs were fully nude, with a reputation for being raunchy.

He came to his feet. ''Are you sure this is all you want?''

She nodded. ''Will you bring my suitcase in before you go?''

He grabbed his keys and went outside. When he came back, she was standing in the living room. The empty background nearly swallowed her whole, and suddenly he didn't want to leave. Would she be all right by herself? Once again, she looked soft and vulnerable. Nancy Perris. Natalie Pascal. The woman who confused the hell out of him.

The following morning Natalie stood in front of a full-length mirror, assessing her appearance. With clammy fingers, she feathered her shorn hair. She still wasn't used to being a blonde, but her hair wasn't the only significant change. Her body was different, too.

Scanning her lean, almost shapeless figure, she smoothed her blouse. Her breast implants had been removed, but eye-popping cleavage would look ridiculous on her now. Besides, David had insisted on increasing the size of her bust. He'd chosen the doctor, booked the consultation and paid for the surgery. Natalie had merely stumbled along like a witless brunette, doting on his generosity. Not that she didn't think women had a right to endow their bodies, to look and feel more attractive. But pumping up your breasts and squeezing into tight dresses to please a man wasn't the answer.

With an exhausted sigh, she gazed at her haunted reflection. Brave talk for a woman plagued by nightmares. How many times a week would she have to relive the night of the murder? To remember what David had said to her after the shooting? To recall what he'd done? Natalie had been so shocked, so afraid, so mortally wounded, she'd never told anyone, not even the FBI. Not that it mattered. What had transpired between her and David wouldn't change the outcome of his trial.

Still standing in front of the mirror, she frowned at the shadows under her eyes. She'd tried to cover them with a concealer, but remnants of a sleepless night still lingered.

Anxious, she glanced at the clock. Zack would be here soon. They'd made arrangements to meet at ten o'clock. She hated being at his mercy, but what could she do? Complain to WITSEC? Tell them her inspector was domineering and critical? Oh, sure. And maybe while she was spouting off, she could admit that she found him sexually stirring, too. That ought to earn her some respect. No, she thought. She wouldn't involve WITSEC. If she complained, it would be to the man himself.

When the doorbell rang, she nearly jumped. Why did he have to make her so damn nervous?

She answered the summons, and he gave her a polite nod. A silent hello, she supposed. He wore casual clothes: a tan shirt, jeans, a lightweight jacket. He'd also donned a pair of sunglasses. She would prefer to see his eyes. She had the feeling he was scrutinizing her, checking her out beneath the dark shades.

"Ready?" he asked.

She lifted her chin, hoping she appeared more confident than her pounding heart allowed. Natalie kept telling herself that she wasn't a fraud, but suddenly the idea of going to college seemed a bit too ambitious for a girl who'd barely gotten through high school. "Yes, I'm ready."

He lit a cigarette, drawing hard and deep. "Then let's go."

She led the way to his car. David had been a smoker, too. "That's a nasty habit."

"What? This?" He exaggerated his next drag. "It keeps me sane."

"It'll probably kill you someday."

"Beats being crazy."

By the time they arrived at the Workforce Training Center and picked up a catalog, Natalie decided that having a lawman as an escort wasn't so bad. He wasn't the nicest guy in the world, but at least he was armed. Somewhere on his body, he carried a concealed weapon. Was it under his jacket? Holstered to his belt? She'd heard deputy marshals were taught to shoot from the hip. David used to enjoy discussing firearms. Guns were his passion.

"Do you want to see NIC's main campus?" he asked.

"Sure." She was curious about North Idaho College, even if the classes she attended would be at the Workforce Training Center.

On the drive to NIC, Zack smoked another cigarette. Natalie spotted the Factory Outlets Mall, but wasn't about to bring it up. She didn't want to spar with him again about her clothes. Already the notion of shopping with him weighed heavily on her mind. She would prefer to visit the mall on her own. Of course that meant giving up the comfort of his gun, but she would have to get used to that sooner or later. Zack wasn't her bodyguard. He wouldn't be living on her doorstep.

"When are you going to help me find a car?"

He stopped at a red light. "Getting antsy to get back on the road?"

"Who wouldn't be?"

Before the light changed, he snuffed out his cigarette. "What did you drive in your former life?"

"A Mercedes."

"Let me guess." He turned to study her, then removed the dark glasses. "An SL500 convertible." He glanced at the fancy buttons that adorned her blouse. "Silver, with a set of chrome twenties." When she crossed her arms, his lips tilted in a barely there smile. "What can I say? It's a gift."

Natalie shifted in her seat. The fact that he'd just described her last car, right down to the custom, twenty-inch wheels, set her on edge. What else had he figured out about her? "David didn't buy it for me. It was leased."

"Meaning what? That you got a new convertible every couple years?" He chuckled and crossed the intersection. "I think I'll outfit you in a rusty old Pinto."

She refused to laugh, to appreciate his sardonic sense of humor. "And I think I'll outfit you with my fist up your nose."

He had the gall to grin. "Now that I'd like to see."

Me, too, she thought, as they arrived at the college.

Five minutes later, Natalie walked beside him, impressed by the spectacular view. NIC's main campus was located on the shores of Lake Coeur d'Alene and the Spokane River. "This is nice."

"The tuition is affordable, too." He glanced her way. "Do you want to find a shady spot and look through that catalog?"

She agreed, even though she hadn't realized that she'd brought the class schedule with her. Silent, they headed toward the nearest shore. The weather was warm, the breeze light and clean. The water stretched for what seemed like an eternity.

He chose a patch of grass beneath a tree. Overall, the campus was quiet, but she assumed summer sessions drew less students. She sat on the ground next to Zack, wondering if he ever picnicked by the lake. The last outdoor activity Natalie had planned had been on the day of the murder, the day David had destroyed her.

Zack moved closer. "Let's take a look."

Caught off guard, she opened the catalog. Suddenly she could smell his cologne, a musky scent mingling with the elements.

"How about this?" He pointed to a workshop geared for writing a business plan. "And this?" A financial strategies course.

Natalie turned the next page. "All of these classes seem important," she said, hoping and praying she could pull this off. In her mind's eye, she could see the boutique she intended to open. She'd dreamed up every detail, yet deep down she was afraid of failing, of discovering that she'd gotten in over her head. "Did you go to college?"

He nodded. "I have a degree in criminal justice."

"Oh." Did she think a WITSEC inspector would be uneducated? Someone she could relate to? "How old are you?"

"Forty."

She studied his profile. He was the same age as David, but David covered the gray in his hair and worried about the crow's-feet that had begun to form at the corners of his eyes.

Zack leaned into her, his shoulder brushing hers. "They must have a training program of some sort. A group of classes—" He flipped through the catalog. "And here it is. Check this out. Twelve three-hour sessions on Wednesday nights, with just about every course you'll need."

She read the program outline. It did look promising. "The first class starts next month."

"That's perfect, don't you think? You'll have some time to settle in before you start school."

Touched by his enthusiasm, her heart made a girlish leap. She couldn't remember the last time someone had supported her endeavors. He lifted his head to look at her, and she realized how close their faces were.

Close enough to kiss.

When she lowered her gaze to his mouth, he scooted back, and a blast of shame nailed her straight in the chest. He handed her the catalog, and she summoned the courage to ask the dreaded question. "Are you married, Zack?"

"What? No." He flinched, then frowned at her, an expression that made him seem tougher than he already was. "I'm divorced."

"Recently?"

"It's been four years."

"Was it a bitter separation?" she asked, a bit too curious for her own good.

"Bitter?" His frown deepened. "Are you kidding? It was friendly as hell. Especially after I threatened to shoot her lover's balls off."

Natalie nearly swallowed her tongue. "She cheated on you?"

His gaze locked on to hers. "It happens."

The way it had happened between her and David? Was Zack comparing his situation to hers? Blaming her for being the other woman? Did he empathize with Ellen Halloway?

Natalie tore at a blade of grass. Surely Zack knew that David's wife was responsible for putting a hit on her. Ellen had forgiven her husband, but she wasn't about to forgive Natalie for turning him over to the police. Or for occupying his bed.

Should she explain? Try to make Zack understand?

She gazed at the lake, at a boat bobbing in the distance. "I didn't know David was married. Not at first. When he talked about having family commitments, I thought he meant the West Coast Family. He never mentioned Ellen. Or his children."

"What did you do when you found out?"

"I left him."

He gave her a startled stare. "You did?"

"I called an old friend and started sleeping on her couch. Then I pounded the pavement for a job. I didn't have any skills, but I knew I could work at a clothing store. I've always had a good sense of style."

"So that's when you worked in retail? I thought it was before you met Halloway."

"No, it was after."

"For all the good it did." Zack reached for a cigarette, then cursed when his lighter wouldn't ignite. "You went back to him. When things got tough, you quit your job and took the easy way out."

"None of it was easy." She fidgeted with the catalog on her lap. "But yes, I went back to David."

"Even though he was still married?"

"He told me that he was going to leave Ellen someday. When his children were older, when he could avoid a messy divorce."

"And you bought that? A smart lady like you? Sounds like you were making excuses to stay with him. To hold on to that lifestyle."

"Does it?" She glanced away, hurt by his unwillingness to believe her. And afraid, so deathly afraid, that he could be right.

Three

———

After Zack and Natalie left NIC, he took her to a furniture store, and now he stood in the middle of a mock living room, wondering what had come over him. He'd just met Natalie yesterday, and today he'd told her about his divorce. He'd admitted, without the slightest reserve, that his wife had boffed another man.

"What do you think of this?" she asked.

He turned to see her admiring a contemporary leather sofa, plumped with faux-fur pillows.

She reached for the tag. "It comes in ivory and black. I prefer the ivory, don't you?"

He moved forward, wishing he'd had the sense to keep his mouth shut, to keep his private life private. "It's twelve-hundred dollars."

"I know. Can you believe it? At that price, I should get the love seat and the matching chair, too."

He could only stare. "The love seat is nine hundred bucks. And the chair and ottoman are another grand."

She looked up. "So?"

"So get a grip." Had she forgotten that WITSEC had put a conservative cap on her moving expenses? Or that a figure from the Bureau of Labor Statistics determined the amount of her monthly allowance? This wasn't a high-dollar gig.

"Just imagine how it would look in my house."

Zack shook his head. He'd had to discourage this kind of spending before. Career criminals didn't have a clue. They didn't know how to make their stipend last. And neither, apparently, did Natalie. "I already warned you about being on a budget."

She ran her hand over the top of the sofa, caressing the upholstery with a lover's touch. "This is Italian leather." On a moaning-type sigh, she plopped her butt down, wiggling into the cushions. "You should feel how soft it is."

He wasn't about to get orgasmic over a piece of furniture. "How about this?" Attempting to redirect her focus, he walked over to a couch he'd spotted earlier. A simple, durable design with a three-hundred-dollar price tag. "It's almost the same color."

She followed him, making a disgusted face the entire way. "That's taupe, not ivory. And I want leather."

"By the time you throw in some tables, lamps, a TV, a DVD player, a stereo and the rest of your bedroom outfit, you won't be able to afford a twelve-hundred dollar couch. Let alone a love seat and matching chair.''

She crossed her arms, but somehow she still managed to look pretty—long and lean and feminine.

''Don't pout,'' he told her.

''I'm not,'' she argued.

Okay, so maybe she wasn't, but her lips were full and thick, glossed like sugar-glazed cherries. And to make matters worse, he couldn't remember the last time he'd indulged in dessert.

She glanced back at the ivory sofa she'd caressed, her voice wistful. ''I want that.''

And he wanted to find out if she tasted as good as she looked, but beggars couldn't be choosers. ''I already told you. You can't afford that.''

''I'll use some of my own money. In fact, I'll pay for all of it myself. I'll buy my own furniture.''

''Bad idea.'' He took her arm and guided her away from a salesman who'd been watching them. Or watching her, he should say. The old guy couldn't keep his eyes to himself. ''You have a business to consider, Natalie. You've got to get your priorities straight.''

She didn't respond. She just gazed at him with disappointment in her eyes. And suddenly she reminded him of a wounded child. A street-smart little girl who wasn't so smart.

He moved closer, close enough that no one could overhear. ''How old were you when you met him?''

She blinked. ''What?''

"Him. Lover-boy."

She tucked her hair behind her ears, fussing with the Goldilocks strands. "What does that have to do with a couch?"

"Just answer the question."

"I'm not discussing this here."

"Then I want the whole story when we get back to your place." The truth, he decided. Not the rumors. Or the pieced-together profile he'd read in her file. "I can't help you if I don't know who you are."

"They already made me talk to a psychologist."

"Where you probably lied through your teeth."

She turned away, and when she marched back over to the leather sofa, he almost gave in and let her buy the damn thing. Almost, he thought. But not quite.

Once she realized she'd lost the battle, she refused to shop for the rest of day. Zack ignored her temperamental attitude and took her straight home, intent on having the truth-versus-rumor conversation.

The moment, the very second he pulled into her driveway and parked the car, she leaped out, determined to ditch him. He had to give her credit for trying, even if she didn't have a chance in hell at out-maneuvering him.

He caught up with her and took the keys out of her hand, unlocking the front door and gesturing for her to go inside. She made a beeline for the kitchen and started making the noisiest pot of coffee he'd ever heard, slamming cabinets in her wake.

"I take mine black," he said.

"Well, bully for you."

He leaned against counter. "I'm just trying to help." Trying to understand her, he thought.

"I don't want to talk about David."

Zack moved to stand beside her, to take the glass carafe out of her quaking hands. "He hurt you."

She turned to face him. "He made promises he didn't keep. So what? Your wife did that to you, too."

He ignored the emotional dig, the familiar jolt of pain it caused. "Just tell me how old you were when you met him."

"Seventeen."

"Son of a bitch." Zack searched her gaze, probing deeper. "Did he touch you? Did that bastard—"

"No." Uncomfortable, Natalie stepped back. Did he have to look at her like that? Did he have to make her feel like a victim? "David and I didn't start dating until I was eighteen."

"But you met him when you were underage?"

"Yes." She took the carafe back, determined to keep busy, to make the coffee her system needed. How many postnightmare days could she survive without turning into a zombie?

"Was it at one of his strip clubs?"

She nearly spilled the water. "Who told you that?"

"Is it true?"

She nodded, ashamed of the girl she'd been, of the woman she'd become. "I auditioned to be a dancer."

"How? With a fake ID?"

The coffee started to drip and a fresh-perked aroma filled the kitchen. "I had a girlfriend who worked there, and she helped me get an ID and set up the audition. I was only trying to pass myself off as eighteen. Fully nude clubs in California don't serve alcohol, so they hire younger girls."

"I'm aware of the strip-club ordinances in your state. I know the difference between topless and nude."

Natalie shifted her stance. She was practically pinned against the counter, with Zack watching every move she made.

"What happened?" he asked.

"My ID passed, at first anyway." Images of the past clouded her mind. Images of being alone on a stage, of her heart pounding its way out of her chest. "The club was closed, so all I had to do was audition for the manager. He seemed rushed, like he had a lot going on that day. He'd barely glanced at my phony license." She paused to take a breath. "In the middle of my act, another man came in. It was David, but I didn't know he was the owner. He was standing in a dark corner. The only thing I could see was the tip of his cigarette."

"Did you finish taking off your clothes?"

"Yes." The coffee was almost ready, but she didn't reach for a cup. Her hands were clammy, her pulse erratic. "My girlfriend had been coaching me, teaching me what to do. I thought I was prepared." But she'd been wrong. So very wrong. "I danced to the music and strutted along the tip rail. I even straddled the pole. I was naked, wearing a pair of four-inch heels and praying for it to end."

He remained where he was, studying her with an intense expression. "Why'd you do it?"

"For the money, for a means to be self-sufficient. My mom was always kicking me out of the house. Half the time I had a place to live and half the time I didn't. She used to bring home these really trashy guys, street-hustler types, and if they started checking me out, talking about how pretty I was, she'd blame me."

"So you went to the nearest strip club and applied for a job?"

"What else was I going to do? Turn my mother in to social services? This was Hollywood, Zack. I grew up on the boulevard."

"Tell me about the rest of the audition. What happened after you put your clothes back on?"

"The manager said I wasn't ready, but that I could come back and try again. He told me to work on my moves, to loosen up. Then David came out of the shadows." She could still recall the way he'd carried himself. His strength. His power. "He asked to see my ID, and suddenly I got scared. I wouldn't show it to him. I grabbed my purse and split."

Zack turned to pour the coffee. He handed her a cup and took a sip of his. Grateful for the interruption, Natalie doctored hers with milk and sugar.

"When did you see Halloway again?"

"A few days later. I was hanging out in front of a sandwich shop near the Wax Museum, panhandling with some other kids, and this Jaguar pulled up. No one paid much attention. We were used to seeing expensive cars."

"How convenient for Halloway. Just running into you like that." Zack's tone indicated his disgust. "You know damn well he tracked you down. He went looking for you."

Natalie tasted her coffee. What Zack said was true, but at the time, she hadn't considered the possibility. She'd chalked up the panhandling encounter to chance. "David gave my friends some money and offered to take me to lunch."

"Did you know he was a mobster then? Or did you find out later?"

"I knew. My girlfriend already told me that Denny Halloway's son owned the club. David wasn't as well-known as his father, but he was earning a reputation."

"As what? A pervert? You were seventeen, and lover-boy was what? Twenty-seven? Twenty-eight?"

"You're eleven years older than me," she pointed out.

He gave her a tight look. "What's that supposed to mean?"

"Nothing." Wishing she'd kept her mouth shut, she gulped the hot drink and felt it burn the back of her throat.

He didn't let it go. "Are you comparing me to him?"

"No."

"Yes, you are."

"No, I'm not."

"Bull."

She tightened her fingers around the cup. "It's just the age factor." And his commanding personality, she thought. The way he made her knees weak and her nipples hard. "I wouldn't compare a deputy marshal to a mobster."

"I sure as hell hope not." He trapped her against the counter again, watching her the way a spider watched a fly. "What drew you to him? What was it?"

The same things that drew her to Zack, she thought. The same overpowering ingredients that lured her into his web. "He gave me a place to stay whenever my mother kicked me out."

"He was just trying to get into your pants. Pulling the friend routine until he earned your trust."

And what was Zack doing? she wondered. What was the deputy marshal's agenda? "I thought he loved me."

"He sure had your number."

Natalie wasn't about to disagree. She'd been putty in David's hands. Or Play-Doh, she supposed, considering how young she'd been. "Love stinks."

"Amen to that."

She set her coffee aside, and he drained his cup and put it in the sink. "I guess you've been there," she said.

He shrugged, and she wondered if his heart had turned cold, if he hated the woman he'd married.

He reached into his jacket for a cigarette. After shaking one from the pack, he stuck it in the corner of his mouth. "Can I smoke in here? Or do I have to go outside?"

She almost gave him permission to light up, then thought better of it. David used to smoke in the condo he'd provided for her, but this was different. She had a voice now. She didn't have to cater to a man's needs. "Outside."

"That's what I figured." He headed for the French doors that led to the barbecue deck.

Natalie followed, although she wasn't sure why. Maybe she needed some air. Or maybe she just wanted to question him the way he'd questioned her.

They stood on the redwood planks, the sun at their backs. The lighter Zack had struggled with earlier ignited on the first try, and he lit the cigarette and inhaled.

"What's your ex-wife's name?" she asked.

He gave her a pissed-off look and she wondered if smoke was going to come out of his nose.

"Who the hell cares," he said.

"I do."

"You're just trying to pay me back for interrogating you."

His observational skills annoyed her, but she figured it was part of his training, part of his lawman's psyche. "Why do you have to be such an ass?"

When he raised his eyebrows at her, she knew she'd gotten his goat. Score one for the mistress, she thought.

"Her name is Ida."

"Ida?"

He nodded. "Ida-Humped-Another-Guy."

Natalie couldn't help but laugh. Trust Zack. "You did?"

He laughed, too. "No. Ida did."

"Is that really her name?"

"Truthfully?" He flicked his ashes. "It's Raquel."

Suspicious, she tilted her head. "For sure?"

"Yep. That's her. Mrs. Wreak-Hell."

"Knock it off." Without thinking, she took a playful jab at his shoulder.

He grinned and nudged her right back, knocking her off balance. She regained her footing and realized they were flirting. He seemed to realize it, too. All too quickly, they both sobered. And then neither of them could think of anything to say. Not a single word. Just awkward silence.

Unsure of what else to do, she sat in a patio chair, grateful the deck was equipped with a place to sit. Her legs had turned rubbery. Up until this point, she hadn't considered that Zack might actually want her the way she wanted him.

Like the chain-smoker he was, he finished his cigarette and lit another. Natalie shifted her foot and gazed at the strip of dirt where he'd discarded the filtered butt. Aside from the redwood deck, her backyard contained a small patch of grass and a flower bed scattered with weeds. Should she snap at him for littering her yard or just let it go?

"Her name really is Raquel," he said.

Natalie sighed. "I'm not in the mood for another joke."

"I'm not kidding around." He settled into the chair across from her, his voice as tense as his expression. "I came home early from a business trip and caught her in bed with one of her co-workers. Some pansy-ass Realtor. I met him a few times at her office, but I didn't have a clue. I didn't suspect a thing."

Which must have blindsided him, she thought. Considering his observational skills. "I'm sorry."

He blew out a stream of smoke. "I thought I had a decent marriage. I thought things were okay."

"It's strange how we only see what we want to see." She thought about the night David had killed his associate. The night he'd called her a whore. "How long were you married?"

"Ten years." He turned to study her. "How long have you been having nightmares?"

Everything, including her heart, went still. She hadn't told anyone about the nightmares. Not another living soul. "I don't know what you mean."

"You didn't sleep last night."

"That doesn't mean I have nightmares."

"You have circles under your eyes."

"Being around you is exhausting."

"And being around you isn't?" He took a drag of his cigarette. "I've never seen anyone act like such a baby over a couch."

Suddenly she wanted to kick him, to nail him right in the shins. "I'm sick of men telling me what I can and can't have." David had decorated the condo she'd lived in, insisting on buying antiques, even though old furniture gave Natalie the creeps.

"Well, bully for you," he said, tossing her own words back in her face.

"This is my house, Zack. I can make you leave."

"And I can get the extra funds for a leather sofa."

She narrowed her eyes. "That's bribery."

He flashed a smug grin. "I said I *could*. I didn't say I *would*."

Natalie glared at him, wondering how she could make his life miserable. Then she decided his life was already miserable. He'd caught his wife in bed with another man. "Don't take your Raquel problems out on me."

His smile turned sharp. "Likewise with Halloway."

Was that his way of trashing her? Of reminding her that she'd spent the last decade with a married man? "Why don't you just burn me at the stake? Or better yet, turn me over to David's wife?"

Zack cursed beneath his breath. "I never said that what you did was punishable by death."

Yeah, right. "This from the man who threatened to shoot the other guy's balls off?"

"That was a gut reaction."

"Heat of the moment?" She stretched out her legs, scraping her boots along the wood. "A crime of passion?"

"I didn't draw my gun."

She gave him a level stare. "But you wanted to."

"There are a lot of things I want to do. But that doesn't mean I damn the consequences and do them."

Of course not, she thought. He was a deputy U.S.

marshal, an upstanding, law-abiding jerk. ''What a bore.''

He snuffed out his cigarette and flicked it in the dirt. ''I've had some pain-in-the-ass witnesses, but you take the cake.''

''Get out of my house.''

''Come over here and make me.''

Was he trying to humor her? Trying to make her laugh? ''You owe me that couch, buster.''

''Dream on, lady,'' he said, before he sent her a devastating wink and rose to leave, making her feel like a love-starved teenager all over again.

Four

A few hours later, Zack returned to Natalie's house. When she didn't answer the bell, he imagined her looking through the peephole and ignoring him purposely. But since he didn't hear any footsteps coming from inside, his theory didn't quite fly. What he did hear, he realized, was the sound of running water.

Curious, he followed the sound to her backyard. Just as he opened the gate to call her name, the water noise intensified. Natalie stood with her back turned, adjusting the nozzle on a hose, spraying the deck.

Like the dog-of-dogs, he decided to keep quiet, to take a minute to watch her. She'd changed into a pair of shorts and a tank top. Her legs were a mile long, and the shorts rode just below her rear.

Talk about buns of steel, he thought. This woman was no stranger to the gym. She had the kind of body—

She turned suddenly, then let out a shriek designed to wake the dead. The hose in her hand went haywire, spraying the bottom of his trousers and soaking his shoes. He cursed and jumped out of the way.

She cursed, too. "Damn it, Zack! You scared me!"

He eyed the hose, not trusting her not to aim it deliberately this time. Already his loafers felt like rain-soaked galoshes. "You didn't answer the door."

"So you just came through the gate without saying anything?"

"I didn't get the chance to tell you I was here." Because he'd been too busy checking out her rear. Not that Deputy Dog was the least bit inclined to admit it. "I ordered that couch."

Suspicious, she squinted at him. "You did not."

"I did so." He removed his shoes and peeled off his socks. It was a good thing he didn't have to be in court this afternoon. On occasion, Zack kept extra clothes and an overnight bag in his car, but he hadn't been commuting today.

She turned off the water. "Did you order the love seat and chair, too?"

He gave her an incredulous look.

"It doesn't hurt to ask." She glanced at his trousers and stifled a giggle. "Sorry about that."

"Ha. Ha. Funny girl." When he realized her gaze was aimed at his fly, he bent his head and saw the water spots that started at his zipper and continued to his waterlogged hem.

She bit her lip, and he knew she was doing her damnedest not to laugh. "Looks like you peed your pants."

Yeah, if he were a racehorse. "A towel would be nice. And don't you dare say that you don't have one." He recalled stocking her linen closet with the generic white variety.

"You better not be lying about the couch."

"*Natalie.*"

"Okay." She darted inside, probably laughing her tight little ass off.

When she returned, she tossed a towel at him. He caught it and noticed she wasn't wearing a bra. Her nipples were standing at attention.

"What inspired you to hose down?" he asked, thinking he could use another shot about now.

She pointed to the flower beds. "I was pulling weeds and got dirt on the deck." Moving forward, she cocked her head. "What inspired you to order the couch?"

Zack shrugged. He couldn't explain why he'd done it, not even to himself. He supposed he'd begun to like Natalie, in an annoying kind of way. He tried not to get closer to his witnesses than regulations permitted, but he was only human. Last year he'd relocated another witness associated with the West Coast Family, an ex-con who'd ended up earning his respect. The guy had gotten his life together and married a sweet girl. Zack had been his best man at the wedding. Things like that mattered.

On the other hand, he didn't make friends with his

witnesses, not to the point of chumming around with them. He was simply there to help, to give them the chance to start over. Or to send their sorry butts back to prison, if need be. He never knew which way the tide would turn.

"Is the couch a peace offering?" she asked.

He raised his eyebrows. "Piece?"

"Peace."

"That's what I said." He would have chuckled at his own deranged wit if Natalie, the hot-tamale mistress, didn't have an innocent side. It still bothered him that Halloway had taken advantage of her when she was young. "Just accept the stupid thing and leave it at that."

"Does this mean I'm going to have to scrimp on the rest of my stuff? I was kind of hoping for a big-screen TV."

"You're pushing your luck."

"I'm just kidding."

She gave him a dimpled smile and he hoped he wasn't being conned. He didn't recall her having a dimple before.

Did she know how to control it, to make it appear at will? Just for good measure, he threw the dirty towel at her. "I'm going to scrimp on your car instead."

"You were going to do that anyway."

"Yeah, but now I really am." He took satisfaction in the way she balled up the towel, making a face that didn't include the conniving dimple.

"Do you have parents, Zack? Or were you hatched?"

Clever woman. Smart mouth. Quick mind. "It was a live birth."

"Give them my condolences."

"I can't. My dad's dead, and my mom has Alzheimer's."

Her eyes went wide. "I'm sorry. I didn't—"

"It's okay. I'm used to it. Besides, my mom's a great lady, even if she can't remember who I am most of the time."

"Hmm." She studied him for a moment. "Can't say I blame her."

A smile tugged at his lips. Natalie's sense of humor was as rotten as his. "Keep it up and I'm taking the sofa back."

The dimple returned. "I'll be good."

"Damn right you will."

Her expression softened. "I really am sorry about your parents."

"I barely remember my dad. He died when I was five." Zack wasn't sure why he was telling her this, other than he felt the need to say it out loud. "But I remember the day my mom found out he wouldn't be returning from Vietnam. A navy chaplain came to our door, and she started shaking before he got the words out."

"Your dad died in the war?"

Zack nodded. "He was twenty-six years old, the love of my mother's life." And what hurt most of all, he thought, was that his mom could no longer remember the man she'd married. "She used to talk about him all the time."

Natalie remained where she was, still clutching the towel. "Do you resemble him?"

"Actually, I do." He sent her a foolhardy grin. "Handsome bloke that I am."

She shook her head, and he quit smiling. When they both fell silent, he wished she were wearing a bra. His gaze kept straying in the direction of her breasts.

"Did you grow up in this area?" she asked.

He focused on her face, on those smoky eyes. "No."

"So you're not from the Coeur d'Alene tribe?"

Her question surprised him. He hadn't expected her to zero in on his Indian blood. "I'm part Sioux. The Oglala Lakota Nation," he clarified.

"Really?" She seemed intrigued. "Were you raised on a reservation?"

"No." He sensed this conversation was headed in a direction that made him uncomfortable. "I'm more white than Indian."

She gave his tanned skin a curious observation. "Don't you like being Native American?"

"I didn't mean it like that." He wondered what the hell he was doing, standing barefoot on Natalie's lawn, discussing his heritage. "I live and work in a white world. It's what I know."

A strand of her hair blew across her cheek. The weather was cooling off, the sun less prevalent. "Sounds like you're at odds with it."

He made light of his emotions, feigning indifference. "Non-Indians expect you to behave a certain way and Indians expect you to behave another way. All I can do is be me.''

She wouldn't let it go. ''Do you have family on a reservation?''

''Yes, at Pine Ridge, but I was five years old the last time I saw them.''

''When your dad died?''

He nodded. Zack sent a monthly check to a Sioux charity, but that didn't change his status with his father's family.

She blasted him with another question. ''Wasn't there some sort of uprising at the Pine Ridge Reservation? I think I saw a movie about it.'' She paused, a thoughtful look on her face. ''Something the FBI and Marshal Service were involved in?''

He cursed beneath his breath. Natalie had just stumbled upon his worst nightmare. ''You mean the siege at Wounded Knee?''

''That's it. Oh, my goodness. Were you a deputy then? Were you there?''

His stomach clenched. ''I was nine years old.''

''Oh.'' Her cheeks flushed. ''I guess it's been a while since I've seen that movie. I thought it happened in the eighties.''

''It was 1973.'' The year several hundred Indians, led by the Oglala Sioux Civil Rights Organization and the American Indian Movement, occupied Wounded Knee, armed with guns, pride and grievances. The year Zack's white uncle, the deputy marshal he loved and admired, had joined forces with other federal officers to battle the Indians.

She took a step toward him. "Have you ever thought about going to the reservation? Maybe get to know your relatives a little better?"

"It's crossed my mind." But deep down, he was afraid they wouldn't accept him. His uncle's participation at Wounded Knee would always be there, haunting his youth, making him guilty.

Natalie caught his attention again. "I guess it's safe to assume your Indian blood comes from your dad's side."

"Yes. That's a safe assumption."

She heaved a heavy-hearted sigh. "I don't even know who my dad is." Distracted, she knelt to pluck a weed she'd missed. "Not that it matters. Considering the kinds of guys my mom brought home, he's probably a creep."

When she came to her feet, Zack caught a glimpse of the loneliness in her eyes. Natalie wasn't keeping in touch with anyone from her old life. Although witnesses weren't permitted to reveal their whereabouts, WITSEC forwarded letters and arranged phone calls to extended family members, but Natalie had declined that privilege.

Not that he could blame her. "When's the last time you saw your mom?"

"When I turned eighteen. There wasn't any point in maintaining a relationship with her. She never wanted me around to begin with." A soft breeze blew her hair, feathering the golden strands around her face. "Is your mom in a nursing home?"

"Yes." He knew he shouldn't be sharing personal

information about himself, but it was too late to take the words back. "It's a nice facility. We chose it together. Once she was diagnosed with Alzheimer's, we planned ahead."

"You must be really close to her."

"I am, but it's difficult seeing her the way she is." To look through old photographs, he thought. To wonder what his mother's life would have been like if his father had lived.

"Do you want to come in?" she asked suddenly. "I can make some iced tea or something."

"No, thanks." He gestured to his clothes. "I have to go home and change. I have a dinner engagement." A lie, he thought. But it was the only thing he could think to say. Natalie Pascal was a witness, not a friend. And he'd caused enough damage for one day. He grabbed his socks and shoes. "I'll do what I can to find you a car soon. I'll see what's out there, then we can discuss your options and decide on something in your price range."

"Okay. When will the couch be here?"

"On Thursday, but I'll call you tomorrow. We can finish shopping and whatnot."

"Thank you, Zack."

"You're welcome." He walked to the gate and opened it, and when he glanced over his shoulder, he saw her watching him. For a moment, they simply looked at each other. And then he was gone.

Natalie's guest house looked terrific. With Zack's help, her home was completely furnished. They'd shopped throughout the week, gathering odds and ends. At a local consignment shop, they'd found some stylish chairs and a glass topped coffee table to complement the couch. The TV and stereo had come from a discount store, the lamps, pillows and knickknacks from a little place that specialized in candles, brassware and imported gifts. Her favorite item, a sheepskin area rug, wasn't cheap by Zack's standards, but it cost less than the dresses she used to buy and it tied everything together.

And now here she was, on Saturday afternoon, battling anxiety. She sank into the cushions of the sofa, grateful for the Italian-leather comfort. Natalie still wasn't sleeping. Between fear-induced dreams and long, restless fits of insomnia, she found no peace. But worse yet, was the loneliness, the knowledge that she wouldn't be seeing Zack this weekend.

He'd told her to page him if she needed anything, but she couldn't bring herself to do it. What would she say? "I miss your smart mouth, Zack?" or "I don't know what to do with myself when you're not around?" He would think she was pathetic. Or neurotic. Or both.

Definitely both, she decided. After tossing and turning last night, she'd climbed out of bed, taken a long, perfume-scented bath, washed her hair with a for-blondes-only shampoo and proceeded to make herself as attractive as possible. She'd even given herself a pedicure. Just in case Zack happened to stop by. Just in case he paid her an unexpected visit. And that, she thought, was the behavior of a pathetic, neurotic, I-need-my-field-inspector woman.

She picked up a magazine from the coffee table. She'd bought it yesterday when Zack had taken her grocery shopping, then politely informed her that he didn't spend weekends with his witnesses and would see her on Monday. Unless, of course, she paged him.

She glanced at her watch and wondered what he was doing. Having a beer with a buddy? Playing golf? Waterskiing at the lake? She had no idea what his hobbies were. Antsy, she flipped through the magazine. Maybe Zack sat around in his underwear watching TV on the weekends. Maybe he was a big old lazy couch potato.

No, she thought. That image didn't quite fit. He probably went to the shooting range on Saturday afternoons and blasted the hell out of paper targets.

The doorbell rang, sending her into a girlish tizzy. She discarded the magazine and popped up like a preened and polished jack-in-the-box. Her toenails were as red as the coating on a candied apple, and her slit-up-the-side, Hawaiian-print dress had been pressed to perfection.

Who else but Zack would visit her? He was the only person she knew in Coeur d'Alene. Maybe he would offer to take her for a walk on the pier, or maybe he'd come across a car worth looking at.

Excited, Natalie threw open the door, then stared at the trio on the other side. The woman was blue-eyed, with a compact figure, a clear complexion and simply styled brown hair. The toddler attached to her hip sucked on a bottle, and the towheaded boy wiggling beside them grinned around his lollipop.

"Are you Natalie?"

"Yes."

"I'm Carla Nichols."

The name didn't register, but she'd been expecting a tall, dark man with a badge and a keep-me-safe gun. "Carla Nichols?"

"Your landlady."

Natalie wanted to kick herself. "Of course." How could she have forgotten about her young, suburban landlords? "I didn't think you were coming back until next week."

"We returned last night. Sometimes it's easier to vacation at home when you have kids."

The boy with the lollipop made a sweet face, but Natalie suspected he had a set of mischievous little horns under all that innocence. "Your children are beautiful."

"Thank you." Carla shifted the toddler. "Timmy just turned two and Brice is five."

"Would you like to come in?"

"Maybe for a minute." Carla took Brice's sticky hand and led him into the newly decorated home. "Wow. The place looks great. I like what you did with it."

"Thank you." A twinge of pride fluttered around her heart. "Can I get you anything? A soda? Some coffee?"

The other woman shook her head, then gazed at Natalie through curious eyes. "Zack didn't tell us you were so pretty. You could be a model or an actress or something.''

Or something? Like a mistress? Uncomfortable, Natalie didn't know what to say. "I had time to fuss this morning. You know, with my makeup and hair."

"I've been doing laundry all day." The toddler in Carla's arms jerked his bottle, nearly bopping her in the nose. "It's such a glamorous life." She gave a nervous laugh and held fast to her other child when he tried to grab a brass incense holder that caught his eye.

Natalie wondered if the baby would cry if she reached for him. She hated standing here in her slit-up-the-side Hawaiian garb, feeling like an ornament that was as useless as it was pretty. "Do you need any help?"

"Thanks, but I'm fine." The young mother redirected the older boy's attention and rocked the younger one, getting them both under control. "I actually stopped by to invite you to a barbecue tomorrow. Around two."

"A barbecue?"

"Just a little get-together with a few neighbors. It seemed like a good way to round out our vacation. It's a potluck, but you don't have to bring anything fancy."

Natalie had never been to a potluck. At least not this kind. Moms and kids and freshly mowed lawns. Dads flipping burgers and talking baseball stats. It sounded heavenly, just what she needed to feel like she belonged in Idaho. But what kind of impression would she make? The new girl in town? The tall, slim, single blonde?

"You can bring Zack," Carla went on to say.

Yes, she thought. She could bring the deputy marshal. He would lend some credibility to her character. "Thank you. That would be nice. I'd like to meet the neighbors."

"And Steve, my husband." The brunette's laugh sounded insecure again. "But I'm going to warn him about how pretty you are. And tomorrow I'm going to give Zack a piece of my mind for not saying anything to begin with."

Suddenly Natalie wished she were plain, an average person who fit into everyday situations. "Zack doesn't care about the way I look."

This time Carla's laugh was genuine. "Somehow I doubt that. I'll bet he trips right over his tongue. I kept wondering why a gruff guy like Zack would help a female friend move all the way across the country, but now that I've seen you, it makes sense."

If you only knew why he relocated me, Natalie thought. If you only knew who and what I am.

After Carla and her kids left, she panicked. What should she wear to the barbecue? She glanced at her dress, at the opening that revealed her leg. Certainly not this.

She tried to take a calming breath, but nearly hyperventilated instead. What if Zack wasn't available? What if he told her to attend the potluck on her own? She would look like the man-eater of the neighborhood. All of the other women would hate her.

Without wasting any more time, she paged her inspector.

The phone rang three minutes later, and she jumped to answer it. "Zack?"

"Yeah. What's up?"

She gripped the receiver. "What are you doing?"

"Talking to you," he responded in that droll way of his.

"Well, I need you to get your butt over here and take me to the mall. We were invited to a potluck on Sunday and I have to find something to wear." She let out the breath she'd been holding, her heart pounding in her ears. "We have to decide what to bring, too. I suppose we could make a salad of some kind—"

"What's this *we* stuff?"

"I just told you. *We* were invited to a potluck."

"By whom?"

"Carla."

"Your landlord?"

"She and her husband came home from their vacation early and they're having a barbecue with a few neighbors tomorrow. I can't do this without you, Zack." After a moment of silence, her pulse jumped to her throat. Why didn't he respond? "Did you hear me?"

"Yes."

"So are you going to go to the potluck with me?"

"Yes, but I'm at my cabin today."

Which meant what? That he wasn't willing to take her to the mall? "I don't have anything to wear."

When a chuckle sounded on the other end of the line, she glared at the phone. "This isn't funny."

"You bought clothes yesterday. Remember that little boutique next to the consignment store? I seem to recall a rather lengthy shopping expedition there."

"That doesn't count."

"Why not?"

"Because Carla said she was going to warn her husband about me. She thinks I'm pretty, and now she's mad at you for not mentioning what I look like." Natalie blew her bangs out of her eyes. "You owe me a trip to the mall."

"Carla's mad at me? I barely know her."

"How do you think I feel? I need a pair of shorts."

"You have a pair of shorts."

"I can't go to a neighborhood barbecue in those."

"Why not?"

"They're too short."

"They looked good to me." His voice turned low. "Better than good."

Surprised by his comment, she paused. She hadn't expected him to flirt with her. Not now. "Do you think Carla's husband will like the way I look in them, too?" He cursed, and she knew she'd won.

"I'll be there as soon as I can," he said.

"I'll be waiting," she responded, wishing she didn't need him so damn much.

Five

Zack sat on the edge of a planter in the courtyard of
the Silver Lake Mall, wishing Natalie would get her
hind-end in gear. Already, she'd been in and out of
stores, insisting she hadn't found the right outfit yet.
He knew she was nervous about attending a neighborhood barbecue, but how hard could it be to pick
out a pair of shorts and a T-shirt? Impatient, he
checked his watch. The mall was open until nine,
which gave Natalie plenty of hours to keep shopping,
to keep driving him nuts. How many cigarettes could
he smoke to bide his time? How much junk food could
he inhale? Zack was bored to tears. Sometimes being
a security field inspector sucked.

Maybe he should hurry her along, offer his opinion,
convince her to buy something and get the hell out of

here. He entered the store where she was browsing and found her eyeing a pair of long, pleated shorts. Perfect, he thought. They looked like something a typical sub urban woman would wear, which was the style Natalie was hoping to emulate.

"Try them on," he said.

She glanced up. "They're white."

"So?"

"They'll get dirty. And if I get dirt on the seat of my pants, it might draw attention to my butt."

She had a point, he supposed. A strange, overly self-conscious point, but at this stage of the game, he wasn't about to argue. "Then let's find a darker color." He scanned the rack. "How about these?"

"Black is too harsh."

"Then these?" He lifted a plaid print.

She wrinkled her nose. "I'll look like a lumber-jack."

Yeah, right. When was the last time a tall, gorgeous blonde was mistaken for a guy who worked at a saw-mill? He reached for another hanger. "What about—"

Before he could complete his sentence, she gave him a horrified look. "They have stars on them, Zack. Gold stars."

Which meant what? That the fashion police would show up at the barbecue and slap her with a citation? He thought they were kind of cute. He jammed the starry shorts back on the rack, and she shook her head, letting him know he didn't have any taste.

Bored once again, he decided to amuse himself with a rounder of bikinis. She rolled her eyes, and he toyed with a racy red thong. "You ought to wear this," he said, simply to annoy her.

She huffed out a breath. "Don't start."

"Fine." He pressed the itty-bitty bikini to his body. "Then I'll wear it."

She managed a smile. "You're such a dork."

Suddenly he felt bad about baiting her. This was probably the first time she would socialize with people who weren't mobsters, strippers or thugs off the street. "Don't worry about the potluck. You'll do fine."

"What if the other women don't like me?"

"What's not to like?" He reached for her hand and gave it a gentle squeeze. "You're smart, classy and a good conversationalist."

"Really? You think so?"

"Yeah, I do." He knew he should release her hand, but he didn't want to. Her touch sent a spark of pleasure through his fingers, a moonlight-in-Hawaii warmth that had him fantasizing like a schoolboy. She looked like a tropical dream—a long, lean, floral-wrapped angel.

"You confuse me, Zack."

"You confuse me, too." He maneuvered the red bikini into their joined hands. "Go put this on."

Her breath rushed out. "See what I mean?"

"I'm just teasing you." Just letting off a little steam, he thought. Acknowledging the heat between them, flirting as painlessly as he could. "But if it bugs you, I'll stop."

She seemed surprised. "You're giving me a choice?"

"What? You think I'm a dog?" He paused, then

recalled the way he'd checked out her rear. "No, wait. Don't answer that."

Natalie broke into a light laugh. "I think you're growing on me."

He grinned at her. "Like an old rusty Pinto?"

"More like mold." With a sudden burst of energy, she let go of the bathing suit and spotted something across the store that left him standing in her wake.

He watched her circle the display like a vulture, grab the khaki-colored ensemble off the rack and hoard it like her next meal. Thank God, he thought. His shopping assignment was about to come to an end.

Almost.

After scouring the mall to find sandals to match her new outfit, she steered him into a bookstore, where she led him down a narrow aisle and stopped in front of a display. "I want to bring the perfect dish." She thrust a dictionary-size cookbook at him. "Here. You can help me find a recipe."

He frowned at the monstrosity in his hand. "What's wrong with plain old potato salad?"

She set her shopping bags on the floor and gave him a you've-got-to-be-kidding look. "I'm trying to make an impression on these people."

"I thought you were trying to seem average. And what's more average than potato salad at a potluck?"

"You're not getting this." She propped her hands on her hips, preparing to enlighten him. "Looking average and making average food isn't the same thing. Carla said I didn't have to bring anything fancy, but I'll bet you a week's wages all of the other women are going to bring something more creative than potato salad.''

She was overanalyzing every aspect of the barbecue, he thought. Beating the damn thing to death. Yet deep down, he understood her fear, the anxiety of not being accepted, of not belonging.

Zack wondered what Natalie would say if he told her the truth about the siege at Wounded Knee, if he admitted how it had created a love-hate relationship with his heritage. Or that as a child, it made him feel as though he didn't have the right to own his Lakota blood. A feeling that remained with him still.

''You're not helping,'' she said.

''What?''

''You're just standing there.''

''Sorry.'' He opened the cookbook, then glanced at Natalie. How many times at night did she awaken in a cold sweat? He could see the nightmares in her eyes, but he'd seen the same ghostly look in other witnesses' eyes. She wasn't the first, and she wouldn't be the last. But even so, he worried about her. He sensed there was more to Natalie's nightmares than being hunted by the mob. He had his Wounded Knee, he thought. And she had hers, a secret that chipped away at her soul.

She leaned over. ''Check the salad section.''

He scanned the index and found the appropriate pages. ''Do you plan on buying a cookbook or just stealing a recipe?''

''You think I'm a thief?'' A worried crease formed between her eyebrows, an expression that defined her

Girl Scout honesty. "I have every intention of buying a book."

He chuckled, wondering if she was trying to earn a mistresses' merit badge. "Good thing or I'd have to bust you."

"You're not funny, Zack."

"Yes, I am." He bumped her shoulder, and she teetered on her feet. "Admit it, Natalie. You like me. I'm your big bad hero."

She turned to glower at him, and suddenly that notion came back, the need to touch her, to feel his fingertips tingle. And when her eyes, those cougar eyes, locked desperately on to his, he knew she longed to touch him, too.

"You're my big bad pain in the butt," she said.

"But you like me." He shifted his stance, tempted, so damn tempted, to move closer, to ignite the fire between them. "Don't you?"

She moistened her lips, and Zack went hard, every conscious thought traveling straight to his groin. Suddenly it didn't matter that she was his witness. All he saw was a woman. A woman he wanted.

"Yes," she whispered. "I like you."

He lifted his hand to smooth her hair from her cheek, and a man in the aisle next to them raised his voice, correcting his kid. Natalie flinched and reality hit Zack like a fifty-ton brick.

What the hell was he doing?

He stepped back, appalled by his lust. She stepped back, too, and he wondered what she was thinking. He wasn't about to ask.

"What kind of salad?" he asked instead.

"I don't know." Her breath hitched, a sound of distress, of nervousness, of disappointment. "Something different."

"Different?" His mind wasn't on the potluck, but he was trying to focus. He glanced at the book he'd closed. He didn't even remember snapping it shut. "Do you know how to cook?"

"Yes." She tucked a strand of hair behind her ear, the same strand he'd almost touched. "I can make all sorts of things."

"Then fix something you know how to make. It isn't necessary to fuss with a new recipe."

Anxiety edged her voice, vibrating her words. "But I can't think of anything to bring, not to a neighborhood barbecue."

"Potato salad," he suggested.

She almost laughed, and he was grateful her sense of humor was coming back. "You have no imagination, Zack."

Oh, yes, I do, he thought. He could think of thirty ways until Sunday to jump her bones.

"I make a curried chicken salad that's really good," she said. "But most people don't like curry."

"I do."

Her eyes lit up like Christmas trees. "You do?"

"Sure. Why don't you bring that?"

"All right." She gave him a sweet smile. "It has rice and pineapples and—" She stalled and her smile fell. "Maybe I should make a potato salad, too. Just in case. Curry is just so—"

"Different," he provided.

Natalie sighed, her shoulders sagging, her emotions wavering again. "I'm a mess, aren't I?"

"You're just nervous."

"You can say that again."

"You're just nervous."

"*Zack.*" She smacked his shoulder, and they both laughed, breaking the tension.

"Come on," he said. "Let's get out of here."

She grabbed her shopping bags. "And go where?"

"To the market to get the ingredients you need."

"Then what?"

He put the cookbook back on the shelf. "Then I'll take you home."

"Will you keep me company while I make the salads?"

He almost said no, that he had other things to do. But as she waited for him to respond, a hopeful look on her face, he gave in and agreed to go home with her. Because helping her adjust to her new life, he told himself, was part of his job.

Once Zack and Natalie were in her kitchen, she put him to work. He removed his jacket and rolled up his shirtsleeves, and she spotted his gun, holstered to his belt.

"I can't believe you conned me into peeling potatoes," he said.

She picked up a pot, then scooted next to him to fill it with water, to share the sink. "You're the one who kept going on and on about potato salad."

"Yeah. Me and my big mouth."

He slanted her a half-assed grin and she wondered

about his love life. Did he find time to date? To wine and dine female companions? Or had he gotten cynical after his divorce? Surely he found time to have sex. What man didn't prowl his environment, searching for an occasional bedmate?

A little nervous, she moved away from him and unwrapped the chicken. She wasn't sure what had happened between her and Zack at the bookstore. For one crazy, heart-thrilling instant, she'd thought he was going to caress her face, maybe even kiss her.

She turned to study him, to admire the hard, determined angle of his profile. He wasn't denying that they were attracted to each other, she thought. He made jokes about it. Then again, Zack made wisecracks about everything, including his ex-wife. He poked fun at uncomfortable subjects.

"Have you dated since Raquel?" she asked.

Much to his credit, he didn't bat an eye. He rinsed the potato he'd just peeled and reached for another. "Define date."

She put the chicken on to boil. "Dinner. A movie."

"Yeah, I've done that. But I haven't gotten seriously involved."

"Why not?"

"Because women nag." He gave her a pointed look. "And make men peel potatoes."

She opened a can of pineapple and added it to a bowl of brown rice. "I figured you'd say something like that."

"What do you want me to say? That Raquel destroyed my trust in womankind? That I'm afraid of making a commitment, of putting my heart on the line?''

''Sounds logical to me,'' she said.

''Well, it's not,'' he countered. ''It's bull. When the right woman comes along, I'll go the distance. I'll get married again.''

If the floor had opened up and swallowed her whole, Natalie couldn't have been more surprised. ''You would? Really?''

''Most of my associates are married. Happily married,'' he added. ''I'm not going to buy into Raquel's crap that my job ruined our marriage. I'm not taking the heat for what she did.''

She looked up at him. ''It must hurt.''

''Of course it hurts. But that doesn't mean I'm incapable of falling in love again.'' He turned off the faucet and leaned against the sink, his gun resting naturally at his hip. ''Did you know that in the early days, some of the deputies used to bring their wives on security detail? Women in the Marshal Service were in short supply at the time, and when a deputy was assigned to protect a female witness, he would call upon the custodial service of his wife.''

Natalie knew he wasn't talking about relocation. He was talking about twenty-four-hour protection. ''A deputy's wife would stay with the witness?''

He nodded. ''The Marshal Service would pay her on an hourly basis. Of course, there was always a deputy on hand, too. But the wife would pull twelve-hour shifts, seven days a week, for as long as she was needed.''

''That's amazing.''

"My mom went on a few assignments. My uncle, her older brother, was a deputy, and since he wasn't married, he used my mom as a matron."

Fascinated, she tilted her head, trying to envision his family. "When was this?"

"The midseventies. I was just a kid. I wasn't involved."

"Your mom doesn't remember any of it, does she?"

"No." He resumed his task, his voice quiet. "But she wasn't thrilled about it then. She was never the law-enforcement type."

"Is your uncle still with the Marshal Service?" Natalie asked, still caught up in his story, in the people who'd influenced him.

He shook his head. "Uncle Joe died about twelve years ago. But he was proud of me being a deputy."

She moved a little closer. The late-day sun shone through the window, highlighting the gray in Zack's hair, creating a soft, silver sheen. "Is it difficult?"

He glanced up. "Is what difficult?"

"Being an inspector."

"It can be, I suppose." A frown furrowed his forehead. "I know of inspectors who've gone to prison, who got mired in business deals with witnesses." He paused. "I know of another inspector who quit his job to marry a witness. Things happen. People get compromised."

"Getting married isn't being compromised, is it?"

"He fell in love with a witness. That's pretty damn deep."

"What about the witness?" she asked.

"What about her?"

"Nothing." Natalie turned away. She wasn't about to admit it, but she identified with the witness who'd married her inspector. Not to the degree of falling in love, but to the degree of needing him, of getting attached. Zack wasn't her husband, but being around him made her feel safe.

Was it a false sense of security? Maybe. But for now, he was all she had. He was investing his time and energy into improving her life. Granted, the Marshal Service was paying him, but she sensed he went the extra mile for his witnesses. He wanted them to succeed.

"What should I do now?" he asked, interrupting her thoughts.

She smiled. There he stood, with a pot of peeled potatoes, ready to accept his next assignment. "How are you at dicing onions?"

"Bring 'em on."

"You won't cry?"

"Yeah. Right." He tossed his head, touting his machismo, shifting his weight from one foot to the other.

"You're quite a guy." Betty Crocker, she thought, with beard stubble and a gun. She took the potatoes and handed him a bag of onions, grateful, so incredibly grateful, that he was her inspector.

Six

Zack considered himself an experienced people watcher. It was his nature, as well as his job, to observe and evaluate the human race. Not that he had the opportunity to assess beings from outer space, he thought wryly. Of course, since the kids gathered around Natalie were pretending to be Martians, he would give them the benefit of the doubt.

He reached for his beer and took a drink. The barbecue was in full swing, with the aroma of mesquite charcoal scenting the air. Umbrella-covered patio tables provided shelter from the sun, and an oversize ice chest offered a variety of sodas and spirits. The potluck dishes had yet to be served, but chips, peanuts and pretzels ran rampant.

Zack turned to study Natalie, to watch her interact

with an armload of kids. She sat on the lawn, attaching an aluminum foil antennae to a little girl's headband. The youngster waited and wiggled, excited at the prospect of being a real-live alien.

"She's the Martian princess," Natalie said to the other children. "So you can't zap her anymore."

"Who are we supposed to zap?" One freckle-faced guy asked, wielding his fluorescent water pistol like the laser gun it was supposed to be.

"You boys can zap each other," she told him. "But not Princess Jane. She's the only girl here, and she's the ruler."

Impressed by the clever negotiation, Zack saluted Natalie in his mind. Six-year-old Jane, with her frizzy ponytail and missing front tooth, was no longer the minority. Attired with a set of royal antennae, the gawky little girl took on a ladylike air, reigning over a bunch of young, rambunctious males.

"Hey, Zack." Carla approached, snagging the chair next to his.

"Hey," he repeated. "I noticed Brice is part of the alien troops."

"That he is." She shifted to look at her oldest son, who drank from a lime-green pistol, shooting water into his mouth. "What a group."

"Yeah."

Carla reached for a tortilla chip and dipped it into a bowl of salsa. "She's quite a lady."

Zack knew she meant Natalie. "We're just friends."

"So you say." She ate the chip, a matchmaker

gleam in her eye. "I still don't understand why you didn't tell us how pretty she is."

As much as he wanted to squirm, he maintained an unaffected posture. "You've already given me heck for that."

"Well, I'm giving you heck again. When an underwear model moves into the neighborhood, the rest of us plain Janes would like to know about it."

Plain Janes? He glanced at Princess Jane, who was being outfitted with a makeshift scepter, a spindly stick with a ball of aluminum foil at the end. "Natalie isn't an underwear model."

"She looks like one."

Zack knew damn well that Carla was trying to prod him into agreeing with her. Determined to outwit her, he met her gaze. A bit too smug, she sat back and waited for him to come clean, to admit that he had the hots for Natalie. "You're not plain," he said.

"And you're more than Natalie's friend," she challenged.

"No, I'm not."

"You will be. You and Natalie have chemistry." She paused to glance at her husband, who flipped burgers on the grill. "Even Steve noticed it."

Somehow Zack doubted that Steve had offered an opinion willingly. His wife had probably badgered him into it. "You're just trying to pawn Natalie off on the only single guy around."

"She seems like a great catch." Without bothering to excuse herself, Carla rose to help her man tend to the food, leaving the chair beside Zack empty again.

Within no time, the meal was served. Adults, teenagers and children crowded around the grill, then lined up in front of the potluck table. Natalie had put a "curry" note on the chicken salad she'd brought, letting the other guests know it contained the questionable spice. The adventurous eaters dug right into it, and so did Zack. He liked exotic food.

He liked exotic women, too, he thought, wishing Carla hadn't honed in on his hunger for Natalie.

With their plates full, Zack and Natalie sat beside each other. Every so often, their shoulders would brush or their eyes would meet. But because he couldn't think of anything to say to her, he engaged in conversation with the other people at their table.

She chatted, too. A bit quietly, but she still socialized. Zack wondered how she was holding up, if she was starting to identify with her neighbors.

Finally, he leaned into her, catching a whiff of her perfume or lotion or whatever it was. "The curry is good," he said.

"Everything is good." She skewered a marshmallow from her fruit salad and brought it to her lips.

Zack's zipper went tight, and he cursed his lack of self-control. If she were anyone but a witness, he would ask her on a date, then initiate a warm, wet, endless night of—

"Beer?"

Caught off guard, he blinked at the man across from him. "I'm sorry. What?"

"Can I get you another beer? I'm going to grab one for myself."

"Sure." He could use a second drink, he thought.

"How about you?" the friendly fellow asked Natalie. "Need a soda refill?"

"No, thank you."

She blotted her mouth, and Zack's body reacted. When his beer arrived, he twisted the cap and took a long, hard swallow.

At sunset, the barbecue wound down and the guests started gathering their kids and their leftover food containers. Natalie helped Carla clean up, and Zack helped Steve entertain Brice and Timmy. While Brice talked to Zack about cops and robbers and bad-guy Martians, Timmy the two-year-old sat on his daddy's lap, bouncing like a jumping bean.

An hour later, Zack walked Natalie to her door. "You better come in," she said.

"Why?" he asked.

She stood on the stoop, looking soft and sweet in her suburban shorts and preppy top. "You've been drinking."

He glanced at her mouth. Her lips were bare, void of the glossy color she normally wore. "Drinking?"

"Yes, Zack. You know, alcohol."

He snapped out of the trance, determined to take control of his senses. "I'm not impaired. I've had two beers in—" He paused to check his watch. "Three hours. Do you want me to give you an estimation of my blood-alcohol concentration?"

"You can do that?"

"Based on my weight, the amount of drinks I've

had and time frame in which I consumed them? Yeah, I can do that.''

"Oh.'' She fidgeted with her keys. Behind her, dusk had fallen, painting the sky in a rich lavender hue. "You could come in anyway. To visit for a while.''

He knew he should leave, but what difference would another hour make? There was no one waiting for him at home. "I suppose I could.''

He followed her inside, and she put away the left-overs and started a pot of coffee. "Do you want some?'' she asked.

"No.'' Zack rarely drank coffee after the sun went down. "You're addicted to caffeine, Natalie.''

"It keeps me awake.''

"Is there something wrong with sleeping?''

She shrugged, then sighed, her voice barely audible. "I have nightmares. But you already figured that out.''

He searched her gaze and noticed the faint circles under her eyes. The ever present exhaustion, he thought, just below the surface. "Do you want to tell me about them?''

"The nightmares?'' She reached into the cabinet and removed a cup. "It won't help.''

Concerned, he watched her, wondering how long she could function, how long she could keep running on empty. "When's the last time you had a full night's sleep?''

"Since before the murder.'' She waited for the coffee, but she was already jittery, already anticipating her next bad dream. "I wish you could stay with me.''

She spun around, clutching her cup. "Will you, Zack?"

"What?" Confusion pummeled his senses, punching his ribs. If he hadn't been leaning against the counter, his knees would have buckled.

"Will you stay here tonight? Will you sleep on my couch?"

"I—"

"Please. Just this once."

"I can't stop you from having nightmares, Natalie."

"Yes you can. I feel safe with you."

"It's against regulation."

"Please," she said again. "I promise I won't do anything to get you in trouble. I won't tell anyone."

I'm already in trouble, he thought. Major trouble. How could he refuse? How could he abandon her?

"Zack?" she pressed.

He cursed beneath his breath, working out a compromise in his mind. "I'll stay, but only until you fall asleep."

She chewed her bottom lip, analyzing his offer. "What if I have a nightmare after you leave?"

"Then you can page me, and I'll call you back. I'll keep you company on the phone."

"That isn't the same as having you here."

He gave her a solemn look, wishing he could walk away, wishing she didn't matter so much. "It's the best I can do."

"Okay, but I'll make up a bed for you on the couch. Just in case."

"Just in case?" Was she trying to con him?

"It takes me a long time to fall asleep."

"How long?" He eyed the coffeepot with suspicion.

"It depends." She poured herself a cup. "Three, sometimes four hours."

"No damn wonder." He grabbed the cup from her. "No caffeine."

"I'm still making up a bed for you."

"Fine." He knew when to quit arguing with a woman, when to let her think she'd won. "But I'm only staying until you fall asleep."

Natalie tossed and turned and prayed that Zack hadn't left. How would he know when she fell asleep? Would he come into her room? Would he check on her? She glanced at the clock. It was only ten. Much too early for her to settle in, but Zack had insisted. She felt like a child who'd been sent to bed without her dinner. Of course, she'd eaten some of the potluck leftovers. Food wasn't the problem.

Edgy, she pushed away the covers. An amber lamp burned beside her bed, but these days, being in the dark gave her the creeps. Would Zack yell at her if she climbed out of bed? If she got a glass of water? What she really wanted was a cup of coffee, but she knew he would blow a gasket if she started a pot.

She sat up and frowned. Maybe a cup of herbal tea would help her relax. Sooner or later, she would have to force herself to sleep.

Natalie crept down the hall and headed for the kitchen. Stalling for a moment, she listened for the TV and was rewarded with an old western. Apparently Zack hadn't left yet. With a deep sigh, she set about to make her tea, tiptoeing like a mouse.

She got as far as the cupboard. "What are you doing in there?" he called out.

She froze. "Getting something to drink."

He didn't respond. But within seconds, she heard his footsteps. He appeared at the entryway. The light above the stove flickered, giving his features an ominous glow.

"Don't be mad at me," she said.

"I'm not mad." He moved closer. "Did you have a nightmare?"

"I haven't even fallen asleep yet."

"Because you're up gallivanting around. How are you going to sleep if you don't stay in bed?"

She filled a cup with water and put it in the microwave. "I keep worrying that you'll be gone. That it'll happen and you won't be here." She rifled through the tea bags. "I wish you could stay."

He didn't respond. He simply watched her, making her feel like an intruder in her own kitchen. She wondered if he'd ever set a mousetrap, one of those horrible things that nearly snapped the poor critter in two.

"I have a deal to make with you," he said.

Her pulse jumped. "What?"

"I'll stay here tonight, but only on one condition. You agree to see a psychiatrist about your nightmares. You get some professional help."

That was his deal? Sending her to a shrink? "WITSEC won't allow it."

"Yes they will." He kept his eye on her, still assessing every move she made. "I can arrange it."

She lifted the tea bag to her nose, inhaling the mint. Behind her, the microwave timer went off, ringing like the bell in a boxing arena. "I'm not crazy."

"I didn't say you were. But you have to do something about your fears. I can't sleep here every night. I can't protect you from yourself."

Deep down, she knew he was right, but that didn't lessen the knot in her stomach, the nervous energy working itself into a pretzel. "Can I see a lady doctor?"

He smoothed his hair away from his face. Several strands had fallen onto his forehead, slashing across his eyebrows. "If that's what you prefer."

"It is." She dunked the tea bag into her water, then added milk and sugar. Bringing the cup to her lips, she blew on the rim.

"So I guess this means I'm spending the night," he said.

"Yes." She tasted the hot brew, guilty yet relieved. She knew he wasn't permitted to stay with her, and she appreciated his kindness, his genuine concern for her well-being. To her, that was worth a thousand psychiatrists. "I'm sorry I'm such a pain in the butt."

He managed a smile. "You're not that bad."

She smiled, too. "Do you need any toiletries? My electric toothbrush came with an extra head, and there's a bag of disposable razors in the bathroom drawer."

"Thanks. Sometimes I carry an overnight bag in my

car, but I hadn't planned on commuting today." He paused. "You don't mind me using your shower in the morning, do you?"

"Of course not. You can use the bathroom now, if you want."

"Is the extra head in that little storage compartment?"

She nodded, assuming he had an electric toothbrush at home. He took off down the hall, and she remained in the kitchen, sipping her tea. Finally, he came back, with his shirt unbuttoned and carrying his shoes and socks. Apparently he intended to sleep in his jeans.

"Get your ass to bed," he said.

She hugged the tea to her chest. "Can't I stay up with you for a while? You're going to finish watching that movie, aren't you?"

Zack sighed. Natalie looked like a lonely being trapped in the netherworld. A pale pink nightgown flowed to her ankles, and steam rose from her cup, swirling like mist. "I suppose."

"Thank you."

They walked to the sofa and sat side by side. The couch was lined with a sheet and padded with a blanket and a pillow. She finished her tea and set it on the coffee table. He stared at the TV.

She attempted to lie down. Like a pesky little kitten, she kept moving, shifting, trying to find a comfortable spot. She robbed his pillow and half of his blanket. Then her feet landed on his lap.

"Natalie."

"What?"

"If you kick me in the nuts I'm going to be pissed."

"Sorry." She curled her toes and took her feet back. "I won't stay very long."

She pulled the blanket to her neck, and he wished she wasn't so fragile. He knew no one had ever nurtured her, not her mother and not David Halloway.

"Where's your gun?" she asked.

He arched his back. "In my briefcase."

She plumped the pillow. "So it's close by?"

"Close enough for what?" He slanted her a sideways glance. "Hunting down your nightmares and shooting them?"

She nudged his hip with those overbearing feet, and he chuckled. She laughed, too, then closed her eyes.

An hour later, the movie ended. Zack looked over at Natalie and realized she was asleep.

He scooted next to her and stroked her hair, taming the golden strands. "What am I going to do with you?" he whispered.

He opted for carrying her to bed. Lifting her in his arms, he cradled her against his chest. She was tall, but light, a bit too lean for her stature.

Her eyelids fluttered. "What's going on?"

"I'm putting you to bed."

Her head flopped against his shoulder. "Did I fall asleep?"

"Yes." For a moment, he refused to acknowledge the intimacy. He insisted it was just another facet of his job. But as she nuzzled his neck, her skin smooth and soft against his, he called himself a liar.

"Will you stay with me until I fall asleep again?"

"Shh." He elbowed his way into her bedroom.

"Will you, Zack?"

"Yes, now be quiet."

"Don't turn out the light."

"I won't."

He placed her on the bed and she tugged him down with her. They nearly landed in a heap. He removed his tangled shirt and altered their positions, leaning back, allowing her to recline in his arms. She snuggled into him, and he slid his hands down her back and connected with her nightgown. The fabric moved through his fingers like cream spilling from a cup. Wolflike, he inhaled her scent. And got instantly aroused.

Uh-oh. He stilled his hands, held his breath, resisted the urge to press his fly against her stomach.

"You feel good," Natalie said.

His voice cracked. "Good?"

"Mmm." Her words sent a puff of air along his skin. "You're hard... I mean strong." She buried her face against his neck. "Sorry. Freudian slip."

"That isn't funny."

"I said I was sorry. Besides, I was talking about your chest." She skimmed his nipples, almost catching one with her nail. "See?"

His body jolted, his zipper bulging even more. "My chest, my ass."

She blew an irritated breath. "Don't start, Zack."

"Start what?" He was tempted to buck his hips and knock her straight to the floor. He could even imagine her startled little yelp. "You're the one who got us into this mess."

She rose on her elbows. Fire blazed in her eyes. Or was it moonlight? "Me? You're the one who's turned on."

Yeah, but that wasn't his fault. He was in bed with an underwear model. Or the equivalent of one. "Just shut up and go to sleep."

She didn't listen. She stayed where she was, hovering like a ravish-me temptation. "I can't. Not when you're like that."

What was he supposed to do? Dump a bucket of ice down his pants? "At least I'm wearing jeans."

"I can still feel it."

So could he. Zack could feel every muscle react, every cell come to life. "It?"

"Your thing."

"Thing?" he mimicked, making fun of the stupid euphemism.

"You're such a jerk." She tried to pull away, but he grabbed her by the waist, dragging her against the body part in question.

She clawed his shoulders, and they rolled over the bed, hissing like a couple of alley cats. Finally, he pinned her beneath him, and they stared at each other, tempers flaring, hearts pounding.

"Do it," she challenged.

"Why? So you can pound the hell out of me?"

"Try it and see."

"Don't think I won't." Without another word, he crushed his mouth to hers. Her nipples turned hard, hitting his chest like bullets, riddling him with pain, with pleasure, with a need so fierce he nearly lost his mind. God help me, he thought, as she dug her nails deeper into his skin.

God help them both.

Seven

Natalie wanted to devour Zack, all of him, every hot, wicked inch. He thrust his tongue into her mouth and made a desperate sound. She rubbed against him, inviting him to take her at will.

The kiss turned even more feral, tongues and teeth clashing. He licked the shell of her ear and bit the side of her neck; she grazed his stomach and pressed her thumb into his navel.

Breathless, they stared at each other, and then she saw the torment in his eyes.

"Make me stop," he said. "Tell me this is wrong."

Natalie froze, praying it wasn't over before it had begun. "I can't." She wanted to caress his face, to follow the stern angles and hard lines, to shape them with her hands. But she couldn't seem to summon the courage, fearing his rejection.

"Say it," he demanded.

Silent, she remained where she was, her body flooded with warmth. She needed him, and she couldn't bear to let go, to lose the connection.

He closed his eyes, waging his own private war. With a quaking hand, she pressed her palm to his chest and felt the erratic beats.

When he opened his eyes, she took her hand away. A minute passed. Or maybe it was a second. For Natalie, time stood still. Finally, she inhaled a deep breath. "I can't," she said again. "I can't tell you it's wrong."

"Then I'm taking you." His voice turned rough. "I'm taking all of you." He pitched forward to kiss her, to attack her nightgown.

Suddenly his hands were everywhere, questing, caressing, tugging at the silk. She reveled in the glory, in the recklessness, in the knowledge that he wanted her. He sucked on her nipples, one, then the other, drawing hard and deep. Without warning, he slipped his hand down the front of her panties, and she nearly climaxed on the spot.

"You're wet." He breathed against her ear, and she feared she might melt or moan or die a million deaths. Stoking the fire between her legs, he staked his claim. What would he do if she begged for more, if she—

He removed her panties and suddenly she couldn't think. He was sliding down her body, taking what he wanted, giving her what she needed. Natalie fought the air in her lungs, fought the shyness of lifting her hips, of letting him fulfill her deepest, most intimate fantasy.

But she couldn't say it out loud. She couldn't admit that David had never offered to do this to her. That he'd never pleasured her the way she used to pleasure him.

She closed her eyes, and Zack pulled her closer.

Then made love to her with his mouth.

The room started to spin, colors twirling in her mind. His tongue was like a drug, warm and addictive. She rubbed against the pressure, against the wetness, against the white-hot flashes streaking through her blood.

The orgasm hit her like a damp fist, contracting her muscles, making her legs tremble. He held her still, keeping her in place, driving her mad. Gloriously mad.

''Zack.'' She said his name, the name of her protector.

He didn't stop. He laved the moisture from her release, tasting it like honey. She arched her body and moaned. And finally, when he lifted his head and took her in his arms, she drifted on a cloud.

Zack pressed his lips to Natalie's temple. He could feel her heart pounding, drumming next to his. ''Are you all right?''

''Mmm.'' She made a dreamy sound. ''Are you?''

No, he thought. He was so aroused, he could barely think straight. He liked this woman. He liked the way she looked, the way she moved, the way she tasted. ''That was hot,'' he said. ''Sexy.''

She opened her eyes. "Let me do it to you."

He gulped some air, dragging it into his lungs. "I don't think that's a good idea." He stared at her mouth. "I don't think I'd survive."

"Really?" She reached for his fly and undid the snap. "Are you that close?"

His entire body shuddered. He could feel her working his zipper, pushing his jeans and boxers down in one fell swoop. If she dropped her head to his lap, he would lose it for sure. "Not now."

She found his flesh. "Then what do you want to do?"

He pinned her beneath him. "What do you think?"

She only smiled. A siren's smile. The lure of a seductress. Zack knew it was too late to go back, to reason with his libido. He kicked away his clothes and kissed her, as hard as he could.

Within seconds, they were rubbing and growling and purring, swallowing each other's tongues. He figured this was how alley cats prepared to mate. No wonder they screamed so damn much.

Natalie dug her nails into his shoulder, but he didn't care. He wanted her to draw blood. His punishment, he thought. Or his fantasy. At this point, he couldn't be sure. Steeped in her scent, he straddled her. She smelled like a hot summer night, like a cool winter breeze, like flowers, like rain. She confused him; she made his brain spin.

Lifting her arms above her head, he cuffed her wrists with his hands, making her his prisoner. "Please

The Silhouette Reader Service™ — Here's how it works:

Accepting your 2 free books and gift places you under no obligation to buy anything. You may keep the books and gift and return the shipping statement marked "cancel." If you do not cancel, about a month later we'll send you 6 additional books and bill you just $3.57 each in the U.S., or $4.24 each in Canada, plus 25¢ shipping & handling per book and applicable taxes if any.* That's the complete price and — compared to cover prices of $4.25 each in the U.S. and $4.99 each in Canada — it's quite a bargain! You may cancel at any time, but if you choose to continue, every month we'll send you 6 more books, which you may either purchase at the discount price or return to us and cancel your subscription.

*Terms and prices subject to change without notice. Sales tax applicable in N.Y. Canadian residents will be charged applicable provincial taxes and GST.

If offer card is missing write to: Silhouette Reader Service, 3010 Walden Ave., P.O. Box 1867, Buffalo NY 14240-1867

NO POSTAGE
NECESSARY
IF MAILED
IN THE
UNITED STATES

BUSINESS REPLY MAIL

FIRST-CLASS MAIL   PERMIT NO. 717-003   BUFFALO, NY

POSTAGE WILL BE PAID BY ADDRESSEE

SILHOUETTE READER SERVICE
3010 WALDEN AVE
PO BOX 1867
BUFFALO NY 14240-9952

PLAY **Lucky 7** and get **2 FREE BOOKS** and a **FREE GIFT**

Scratch off the gold area with a coin. Then check below to see the gifts you get!

NO COST! NO OBLIGATION TO BUY! NO PURCHASE NECESSARY!

DETACH AND MAIL CARD TODAY!

YES! I have scratched off the gold area. Please send me the **2 FREE BOOKS AND GIFT** for which I qualify. I understand I am under no obligation to purchase any books as explained on the back of this card.

326 SDL DZ4W   225 SDL DZ5D

FIRST NAME	LAST NAME

ADDRESS

APT.#	CITY

STATE/PROV.	ZIP/POSTAL CODE

(S-D-04/04)

Worth **2 FREE BOOKS** plus a **FREE GIFT!**

Worth **2 FREE BOOKS!**

Worth **1 FREE BOOK!**

Try Again!

tell me you're taking the pills I saw in your bathroom drawer.''

She worked free, pulling him closer, branding his skin. "I am."

"Good." More than good, he thought. He didn't care why she was taking birth control pills. For now, all that mattered was thrusting into her. Zack couldn't recall ever being this desperate for a woman, this hungry. She wrapped her legs around him, gripping like a vise. He prayed that she would never let go, that it would never end.

Blood pounded in his heart, echoing in his loins. He lowered his head to flick his tongue over the tip of her breast. She tugged at his hair; he used his teeth.

Maybe they were going mad, he thought. Expelling their fever in one forbidden coupling. His vision blurred, his mind reeled, but he could still see her in the amber light, a wash of pale colors, of long, lean curves.

Fascinated, he watched her. She moved with him, stroke for stroke, heat for heat. He wasn't sure who climaxed first. All he remembered was the urgency, the lash of pleasure, the power of hearing her cry out as he spilled into her, soaking her with his seed.

He fell into her arms and a few quiet moments passed. Finally, she shifted beneath him, stretching and mewling. He lifted his head to look at her, knowing he wasn't any better. He groaned like a grizzly.

She smiled and touched his cheek. "Where have you been all my life, Zachary Ryder?"

He cleared his mind. "Zachary?"

"Zachariah?"

"It's just Zack."

"I should have known." Her eyes were darker without the tinted contacts, but still cougarlike. "Zack suits you."

"And Natalie suits you. It's a glamorous name."

"I'm not feeling very glamorous. I'm all sticky."

"Yeah." He pressed against her. "Isn't sex grand?"

They looked at each other and laughed, and he wondered why he hadn't lost his sense of humor by now. "I'm dying for a cigarette."

She wrinkled her nose. "That's a nasty habit."

"So you've told me." He kissed the tip of her twitching nose, knowing damn well that he would despise himself in the morning. "Are you going to make me smoke outside?"

She bumped his groin. "You think this gives you privileges?"

"A guy can hope."

"A guy can take his bare butt onto the patio and destroy his lungs."

"You're an evil woman." And he was a stupid man. He glanced at his jeans, dreading daylight, dreading the remorse that was sure to set in. "Maybe I'll skip the cigarette."

"Good idea. You can stay here with me instead."

Yes, he thought. He could stay with her. When he reached for her, she buried her face against his neck, nuzzling gently. In turn, he stroked her hair.

"You smell good," he said.

Natalie pressed her lips to his skin, grateful that he cared enough to hold her. She couldn't tell him how much it meant to her. She couldn't bear being treated like a mistress, not by him. "You smell good, too."

"I washed my face with your soap," he mused.

She pulled back a little, just enough to study him. Deep creases shadowed his cheekbones and the lines near his eyes marked his association with the sun. "What's your cabin like?"

"My cabin?" He squinted at her. "What's that got to do with soap?"

"Nothing. I'm just curious." She wanted to picture him in his everyday life, to know him on a deeper level. "So what's it like?"

"It's rustic, I guess. Sort of primitive. There's a creek nearby. Lots of wildlife. It's my home away from home."

"It sounds wonderful," she said, wishing he would invite her to visit him, to be part of his existence. "I like being in the country."

He skimmed her cheek. "I thought you were a city girl."

At this point, she wasn't sure who or what she was. "The idea of commuting appeals to me. It seems like you have the best of both worlds."

"I don't know. Maybe. Sometimes it hardly matters."

It mattered to her. "You're a special man, Zack."

He slid his hand down her spine. "And you're a beautiful woman."

She put her cheek against his chest, listening to his

heart, to the strong, steady beats. She'd been told that all her life, but it hadn't counted until this moment. Being beautiful for Zack was like being reborn.

"Can I do it to you now?" she asked.

His chest rose and fell. "Do you want to?"

She glanced down, saw that he was getting aroused. "Do you want me to?"

His voice turned rough. "Yes, but—"

She didn't let him finish. Instead she thrust her tongue into his mouth and made him groan. "But what?" she asked.

"I'm—"

"Sticky?" she said.

He nodded, but she could see that the idea turned him on. He was being polite, but deep down, he wanted her to taste what they'd done.

She lowered her head to kiss his belly button, to flick her tongue. He shifted his weight, and his arousal strained, brushing her lips. Natalie couldn't help but smile.

He said her name, and she looked up. His eyes were glazed, brewing with intensity.

Empowered, she teased him, licking the salty moisture from the tip. He tangled his hands in her hair, fixated on every move she made.

Setting a warm, fluid rhythm, she took him into her mouth, loving him, stroking him. He cupped her face, and she felt the strength of his need. He moved with her, rocking his body, pushing deeper, making her take more of him.

She relaxed her throat, swallowing every inch, and

his stomach muscles jumped, rippling across his skin. Zack, she thought. Erotic Zack.

On a growl, he lifted her up, dragging her against his body, rubbing flesh against flesh, igniting a fire, adding sparks to the flame. Heat pooled between her legs, slick and moist. Steeped in sensation, she melted like a candle, dripping wax all over him.

More than ready, he rolled over, taking her with him, thrusting strong and deep. Natalie's pulse tripped and stumbled. He kissed her so hard, her heart spun. Bodies fused, they fed on each other, rolling over the bed, bunching the sheets.

He laved her nipples, making them ache, making her long for more. She wanted to suspend this moment, to make it last, but her vision was blurring, her mind twirling like a top. Reality slipped away, the world shifting into a haze of hot, blinding color.

Dizzy, she focused on his face, on those hypnotic eyes. And then she felt herself fall, climaxing in his arms. Within a heartbeat, he followed, claiming her with a warm, drugging kiss.

Disoriented, she held on to him, her limbs turning to mush. With their bodies still joined, he whispered something in her ear, something soft and gentle, something that soothed her into a slow, sweet slumber.

Zack awakened early. He squinted and rubbed his eyes. He hadn't slept well, but Natalie had slept like a dream. A good dream, he thought. She hadn't been plagued by nightmares.

She lay next to him, snuggled under a blanket. He

wanted to touch her, to rouse her with a kiss. But God help him, he couldn't. This wasn't a fairy tale. This was reality—the morning-after. He'd made love to a witness, jeopardizing his career, screwing with her emotions, messing with his.

She stirred in her sleep and the blanket slipped, just a little, just enough to give Zack a glimpse of smooth, creamy skin. She looked so innocent, so vulnerable. He sat up and pulled his hands through his hair, nearly tugging it from his scalp. Of all women, he asked himself, why her? Why David Halloway's old mistress?

With a vile curse, he climbed out of bed. He wanted to go home, to beat his head against a wall, but he knew he couldn't walk out on Natalie. Not now.

An hour later, after taking a shower and brewing a pot of coffee, Zack sat on Natalie's patio deck, smoking his third cigarette. The morning air was mild, the sky a soft shade of blue. Normally, he took comfort in the elements, in birds raising their voices in cheerful song, in the sun filtering through the clouds, but today his soul betrayed him.

Shifting in his chair, he snuffed out his cigarette, flicking it in the dirt. Maybe it was a nasty habit. Maybe he had no right to choke the world with second-hand smoke.

Great, he thought, as he glanced at the flower bed. Just great. Not only was he stressing about giving other people cancer, he was guilty about littering Natalie's yard. Pissed off at himself, he retrieved all of the butts he'd discarded, intending to dispose of them properly.

"Zack?"

Caught off guard, he spun around. Natalie stood on the deck, wrapped in a silky white robe, a cup of coffee cradled in her hands.

Feeling big and boyish and stupidly tongue-tied, he shifted his feet. She smiled, and he wondered if she was naked under the robe or if she'd slipped on a pair of panties.

"Hi," she said.

"Hi," he parroted, managing to find his voice. "Is the coffee okay?"

"Mmm." Her robe gaped, exposing the flesh between her breasts. "It's perfect. I love waking up to freshly perked coffee."

He tried not to look, but his gaze strayed. He should have kissed her when he had the chance, held her, whispered an apology in her ear. "We need to talk."

"About last night?"

"Yes." He fisted the smoked-out cigarettes in his hand, wondering what to do with them. Walking past her to the trash cans on the side of the house didn't seem like an option. Nor did hauling his sorry ass into the kitchen. She was staring at him, waiting for him to expound. He shoved the butts into the front pocket of his jeans and felt the tobacco scatter. "Why don't you sit down?"

"This is bad, isn't it?"

"I broke a major rule."

She took a seat, tightening her robe. Her hair shimmered in the morning light, still tousled from sleep. "That doesn't matter. At least not to me."

He sat, too, then spotted his coffee on the ground where he'd left it. Natalie's patio lacked a table. "It's going to matter to my superiors."

Her cheeks went pale. "You're going to tell them?"

"What choice do I have?" He couldn't hide from the truth. In spite of what he'd done, he was a man of honor. He couldn't go on, pretending that he hadn't slept with a witness.

"What's going to happen to you?" Her eyes grew wide, filled with panic. "To us?"

Zack blew a windy breath. The least he could do was reassure her, keep her calm. "Don't worry about it. They'll still take care of you. They'll—"

"I don't want them to take care of me. I want you. You're my inspector. You're my—"

"Lover?" he provided. "Don't you see? That's the problem. That's where I screwed up."

She hugged her cup, pressing it to her chest, keeping herself warm. "Do you regret what we did?"

"Yes, but I knew I would. I just didn't want to face it last night."

She blinked, and he prayed that she wouldn't cry, that she wouldn't leave him feeling like the worst kind of bastard.

She brought the cup closer. "I don't regret it. But what do I know? I used to dally with the mob."

Zack's chest constricted. He wanted to go to her, to hug her, but he knew that touching her would be a mistake. "I'm going to take responsibility. No one is going to blame you."

"Do you think I was born yesterday?" She rose,

her legs not quite steady. "I know about the rumors. About all the things the mob and the FBI used to say about me." She gave him a level stare. "I'll bet the Marshal Service said it, too."

He got to his feet. "That doesn't matter."

"The hell it doesn't." Without another word, she turned away. And then she walked into the house, leaving him alone with his guilt, with the rumors he still wondered about.

Eight

Natalie hurt so much, she could barely breathe. She dumped her coffee in the sink and twisted her hands together, locking her fingers, unlocking them. To keep herself from crying, she looked around for something to do. She had to keep busy. If she remained idle, she would—

Footsteps sounded on the floor, snaring her attention, making her heart jump. Zack had followed her into the kitchen. She turned, and they simply looked at each other.

"I have to clean the house," she said.

He frowned at her. "Now?"

"Yes." She glanced around the kitchen. Aside from her cup in the sink, the room was spotless. She noticed

Zack had left his unfinished coffee outside. Or she assumed he did, since his hands were empty.

Empty hands, she thought. Empty heart. Did he care about her at all?

"I'll help you," he said.

She took a step back. "Help me what?"

"Clean the house."

She didn't argue. Instead, she shrugged, hoping to appear less affected, less pained by his rejection. She headed for the living room and spotted the bedding on the couch, knowing Zack followed.

The TV was still on from the night before. She picked up the remote control and pushed the power button. The screen went blank and, for a moment, she stared at it.

"I'm sorry," he said.

"Don't." She turned away from the TV. "Don't apologize for something you wished you'd never done."

"It was wrong. We both know it was wrong."

She grabbed the rumpled blanket from the couch and proceeded to fold it. "Then why did it feel so right?"

He went after the sheet. "Because we're so damn attracted to each other. Because—" He paused to snap the material, to pinch the corners together. "If you were anyone else, I'd pursue a relationship with you."

"Pursue a relationship?" She tried to keep her voice calm, praying it wouldn't quaver. Their paths had crossed because he was a security inspector and she was a witness. Nothing would ever change that. It was part of who they were. "What does that mean? That if I wasn't a witness, you'd sleep with me again?"

"Yes, but—" Frustrated, he struggled to form an answer.

She gave him a pointed look. "But what?"

"I have to contend with my job. I have to deal with the consequences." He placed the folded sheet on the couch, stacking it on top of the pillow. "When a security inspector screws up, he either gets fired or transferred out of WITSEC. So even if they let me keep my badge, there's no way they'll allow me to remain in WITSEC. Not over something like this."

"Over this?" Hurt, she fought a wave of anger, of shame, of guilt. "You mean over me? I'm the one who put your job on the line."

"I did it to myself," he countered. "I'm the one who couldn't keep my pants zipped."

"Because I'm an easy lay." She hurled the words at him like a boomerang, feeling like the slut WITSEC would make her out to be. "Isn't that what your superiors are going to think?"

He made a tight face. "They're going to think I made a mistake. They're going to judge my actions, not yours."

"That's bull and you know it. They're going to judge both of us. The deputy with the spotless record, and the mistress who used to go down on David Halloway in public."

Zack flinched. "That's just a rumor." He paused to release an audible breath. "Isn't it?"

Her heart cracked open and bled, spilling like crimson paint. Did he think she completely lacked morals? That she had no self-respect? "Yes, it's a rumor. But it's going to follow Nancy Perris around for the rest of her life."

"You're not Nancy anymore."

"Your superiors know that Nancy and Natalie are one and the same, and my affair with you will prove that Nancy hasn't changed."

"You're asking me not to tell them? To keep what we did a secret?"

"Yes, that's exactly what I'm asking."

"I can't do that."

"Please, Zack." Why was she always begging? Always groveling at his feet? "Don't destroy our lives. Just leave things the way they are. Pretend it never happened."

He didn't respond, and the lapse of conversation left her at odds. Edgy, she turned and walked away. Unsure of what to do next, she tore into her room and started stripping the bed, pulling off the sheets and blankets, dumping them on the floor.

"Can you pretend it didn't happen?" he asked from behind her.

She spun around. How could she sleep here night after night and not think about him? Not relive their lovemaking? "I can try."

"Then I'll let it go. I'll give it some time."

She tilted her head. "Some time?"

"I won't say anything. I won't turn myself in. But if either of us has trouble dealing with this, if we can't cope…'' He let his words drift, then fade into noth-ingness.

''I understand.'' She glanced at the bedding heaped on the floor. Would washing the sheets help? Would it erase his touch from her mind?

''I should go. I have to be in court later and—'' He stalled, indicating his clothes, the pants he'd claimed he couldn't keep zipped. ''I have to get ready.''

She expected him to leave, but he didn't. He re-mained where he was, as though he was waiting for her to respond. She didn't know what to say. Anxious, she fussed with her hair, taming the short, choppy strands.

''When will I see you again?'' she finally managed.

''Soon. Tomorrow or maybe the next day. We need to focus on finding you a car.'' He dug into his pocket, fishing for his keys. ''And I still have to arrange for the psychiatrist.''

She merely nodded. She knew it was too late to back out of the deal she'd made.

''Page me if you have a nightmare,'' he said. ''I can't come over, but we can talk on the phone if that makes you feel better.''

''I'll be fine.'' She wanted to put her head on his shoulder, to reclaim the intimacy they'd lost, but she knew she couldn't. Touching him would only make her ache.

''Are you sure?'' he asked.

''Yes.'' She would drink a gallon of coffee, she thought. She would keep herself awake.

He said goodbye, then turned away. She exhaled a

shaky breath, and when he was gone, when the house was still, she sat on the edge of the barren mattress, missing him already.

After court, Zack visited his mother. Donna Ryder was a medium-boned woman with gray hair and child-like eyes. At one time, her hair had been brown and her eyes a vibrant shade of blue, but she'd lost the confidence Zack remembered so well.

Attired in a yellow blouse and beige slacks, she sat in a rocking chair, painting her short, stubby finger-nails. Zack had brought her the polish. He'd had to explain what to do with it, but he recalled a day when his mother had been fanatical about her nails, mani-curing them to perfection.

"Pretty," she said, gazing at her hands.

"Yes, it is." He met her gaze. She looked so fragile, with her heart-shaped face and scattered mind. "Next time I'll bring you the kind with glitter in it."

"Then I'll be a fairy." Rather than tilt her head, she leaned her entire body to one side, observing him in an odd way. "You're that nice boy who works here."

Zack didn't dispute her claim. There were times when she refused to accept that she knew him at all. At least this was something, some sort of recognition. He reached for the polish while she blew on her nails, drying the pale pink color. Capping the bottle, he glanced around the room. A tan-and-teal bedspread complemented a whitewashed dresser, and a fresh bouquet of flowers presented a springtime aroma.

She'd helped him choose this facility ages ago, when she was still lucid. She still had some coherent days now and then, moments Zack treasured. He missed confiding in her, laughing and talking the way they used to do.

"Are you a fairy?" she asked.

He bit back a grin. He knew she was being serious. Alzheimer's patients often said strange things, and she was no exception. "No. I can't say that I am."

"Do you have a glitter girl?"

He tried not to frown. "You mean a girlfriend?"

"Yes." She finished drying her nails. "A special lady."

He thought about Natalie and his lungs clamped around his heart. "There was someone, but we're not supposed to be together."

"Like Romeo and Juliet." His mother sighed. "I knew you were romantic."

He doubted Natalie would consider him romantic. What he'd done made him a bastard, a user, a guy who'd taken what he'd wanted, then walked away. And worse yet, he was guilty about his job, feeling like a liar and a cheat.

"You're a nice boy."

He studied the disoriented woman across from him, wishing she could remember that he was her son. "Do you want to go for a walk?"

"In the garden?" She rose to retrieve the bouquet on her dresser, cradling the vase like a trophy.

He moved toward her. "You can't take your flowers."

"But they're from the garden."

"They're from a florist shop." He ordered them every week "They're meant to stay in your room."

She made a face and replaced the vase. "You're not a nice boy."

No, he thought, recalling the pain in Natalie's eyes. He wasn't.

He reached for a daisy and handed it to her. "You can bring this on our walk. It matches your blouse."

"It does, doesn't it?" She fawned over the sunny-colored bloom, then took his arm, allowing him to escort her. They passed the nurses' station and proceeded to the fenced yard, where the lawn grew green and lush.

"I love you," he said suddenly.

She stopped walking and blinked at him, her lashes fluttering madly. "You're too young for me. Besides, Juliet is the one who needs you." She patted his hand, consoling him. "It's too bad you're a Montague and she's a Capulet."

"It isn't like that." He reached for a cigarette, fumbled with his lighter. "We're not star-crossed lovers."

"Yes, you are," his mother said before she turned away to look up at the sky, searching for stars in the middle of the afternoon.

As the afternoon sun glared, Natalie shielded her eyes, cupping her hand across her eyebrows. She hadn't seen Zack in two days, and here they were, walking the aisles of a used-car lot in Spokane, Washington. Spokane was close enough to Coeur d'Alene to commute, and Zack had suggested the trip. Natalie supposed there were plenty of automobile dealers in Spokane, considering this was the fifth lot they'd browsed. The outing wasn't going well. When she commented on a make and model that appealed to her, he disapproved, spouting mechanical failures associated with her choices. And when he indicated something he thought would be good for her, she turned up her nose at his practical suggestions.

At this stage of the game, Natalie wondered if they were working against each other purposely, finding excuses to fight, to punish themselves in the process.

"Maybe we should take a break," he said.

"Maybe you're right." She looked into his eyes and saw his discomfort. "You're having a hard time with this."

"We can't seem to agree."

"I'm not talking about cars."

"I'll work through it." He took her arm as an overzealous salesman spotted them. "Let's get out of here." He gestured to an ice-cream parlor across the street. "How about a sundae or something?"

"Are we avoiding the vulture?"

"Yeah. Look at that guy. He's going to start jogging any minute."

Natalie glanced back at the salesman. He was indeed picking up speed, hoping to cut them off at the pass. "Ice cream works for me."

They crossed the lot and made it to the sidewalk in record time. They'd already chatted with a slew of salesmen that day, and they'd had their fill of sturdy handshakes and "take my card" goodbyes.

"Are we being antisocial?" she asked, as they waited at the light.

"I don't know." He shoved his hands in his pockets. "It's a weird day. Maybe it's going to be a full moon tonight."

She looked over her shoulder. The salesman had wandered back to his post. No claws, no fangs. Only an average guy trying to earn a living. "I have a feeling it's just us."

When the light changed, they headed to the ice-cream parlor, a quaint little family-owned place, housed in a brick building. After scanning the menu, Natalie decided on a banana split. Zack stuck with his original choice, ordering a sundae.

After gathering their treats, they occupied a small table. They were the only people seated outside, the scent of a nearby river misting the air.

"This is a nice area," she said.

Zack spooned into his ice cream. As usual, he wore a lightweight jacket that concealed his gun. Strange how an armed man could appear so casual, she thought.

"Spokane means Children of the Sun or Sun People," he said. "But the original spelling didn't contain the *e*."

"I didn't know that." But she was still learning about the Northwest.

"I live here," he told her.

"In Spokane?" She started, surprised that he'd offered information about himself.

He nodded, and she studied his profile. They sat side by side, close enough for her to see the tiny lines that crinkled the corners of his eyes. "So you're a child of the sun?"

"I am now, I guess. This has been home for quite a while." He stirred the fudge that topped his sundae. "I was born in Illinois. That's where my mom is from. She met my dad when he was stationed at the Naval Training Center in Great Lakes."

"Where did you meet Raquel?" Natalie asked, unable to temper her curiosity about his ex-wife.

Zack frowned at his bowl. "Here. She's from Washington."

"Is she pretty?" Natalie asked.

He looked up, and their gazes connected. "You think I'd marry an ugly woman?"

She couldn't help but smile. Zack certainly had a way about him. "No, I suppose not."

He didn't return her smile, and she knew his mind was drifting. When his hair blew across his forehead, she wanted to tame the loose strands, to smooth them with her fingers. But she toyed with her ice cream instead. "Are you sure you're going to be able to work through this?"

"It's not easy for me to lie."

"You lie every day of your life. You give criminals new identities. You send them back into society."

He gave her a level stare. "That isn't the same."

"Why? Because it's part of your job? Because the

government says it's okay?'' She glanced at the road, at the cars passing by. They spoke quietly, even though there was no one around, no one to overhear. ''You're in a morally corrupt business. One criminal goes free so another can be prosecuted. What kind of justice is that?''

''Don't screw with my conscience,'' he shot back, keeping his tone steadier than their conversation. ''I've helped a lot of witnesses over the years. I've watched people turn their lives around. I've seen this program work.''

''And now you're the big bad wolf because you slept with me?''

''I took advantage of my position. Of everything it's supposed to represent.'' He pushed away his dessert. ''And sooner or later, I'll have to do something about it.''

She fought to stay strong, to keep the pain at bay. ''You're going to tell WITSEC about us, aren't you? You're going to admit what we did?''

''They won't blame you, Natalie. I'll take responsibility. I'll explain what happened.''

Suddenly none of that mattered. There was more at stake than her reputation. ''But I'll lose you.'' She lowered her voice even more, bringing it to a whispered pitch. ''You won't be my inspector anymore. I'll never see you again.''

''I won't say anything until you're ready.''

''What if I'm never ready?''

''You will be. Once you've settled into your new life. Once you've spent time with a doctor.'' He reached out to stroke her cheek, to brush his hand across her skin. "Once you can start sleeping again at night."

She leaned into his touch. Did he think it would be that easy to give him up? "But you're my friend."

"No, I'm not. Not in the true sense of the word. I've barely let you into my world. You don't know who I am. Not really."

"Then show me who you are. Let me into your world before I never see you again."

The sun glinted off his hair, like water shimmering in a midnight pool. "Will it help? Will it make you feel different inside?"

"Yes," she told him. It would make their affair seem like something deeper than sex. It would give her the illusion of being more than a mistress, more than the woman who'd compromised an honest man.

Zack drove Natalie to his house, praying he was doing the right thing. A tangle of nerves coiled in his stomach, and he wondered if friendships could be forged from guilt.

She sat quietly beside him, staring out the windshield, reminding him of the day they'd met. He hadn't trusted her then. Did he trust her now?

Yes, he thought. He did. He trusted her smile, the way she laughed, the way she'd looked at him when they'd made love. He glanced at her profile, at the fine-boned features that made her so damn pretty. If she were anyone else, he would let himself feel more for her. But a few ragtag memories were all he could give her, all he could give himself.

He steered the car down a neighborhood rife with cool green parks and towering trees. Zack's house marked the center of a cul-de-sac, giving him the privacy he preferred, with only a few neighbors.

"This isn't where I lived with Raquel," he said. "I bought this place after the divorce."

"It reminds me of the fifties. *Ozzie and Harriet, Leave It to Beaver.*"

He pushed the electronic garage-door opener and waited for the door to rise. Natalie scooted to the edge of her seat, and he sensed her anticipation. "The houses aren't quite that old, but it does have that vibe."

She unbuckled her seat belt. "Is that your truck?"

He parked beside the vintage Chevy. "I'm still playing around with it, restoring it when I have time."

She chewed her bottom lip. "I never pictured you under the hood of an old truck."

"My dad had one similar to this. I guess it makes me feel closer to him." He let out the breath he'd been holding. Exposing his emotions didn't come easily and taking a witness on a tour of his house wasn't something he'd ever intended to do.

They entered through the laundry room, where the washer and dryer presented themselves as typical white appliances. A basket of wrinkled clothes and a box of laundry detergent sat on a nondescript shelf. The kitchen came next, with oak cabinetry and terra-cotta-style tiles. An ashtray on the counter needed to be emptied and a small stack of dishes in the sink had yet to be washed. Other than that, Zack supposed the room was clean.

Natalie's catlike eyes shifted, taking in her surroundings. "It's masculine," she said.

"I'm a guy," he responded.

She turned to meet his gaze. "I know."

They looked at each other, caught in a soundless moment, in naked images, in the lovemaking that had brought them to this point.

Tempted to move closer, to taste what he'd been missing, Zack cleared his throat and retrieved a cigarette, giving his mouth something to do.

As smoke swirled in the air, Natalie fidgeted with her top, a T-shirt that rode the waistband of slim-fitting jeans. He caught a quick flash of her stomach, of the navel he'd kissed.

"Do you want to see the rest of the house?" he asked.

She stopped fussing with her clothes. "Yes, please."

He gestured toward the living room and watched her walk ahead of him. He wasn't sure how long it would take for her to heal from her wounds, from the nightmares she refused to speak of, but he was willing to wait, to give her a chance. He couldn't abandon her until she was strong enough to let him go. For now, she was still his witness, still his responsibility. He'd already jeopardized his job. At this stage, she mattered more than the rules he continued to break.

She stood in the center of his living room, gauging his furniture. "You have a big-screen TV."

"And you have an Italian-leather sofa."

She spun around to smile at him, and he realized they'd already built some pleasant memories, things for both of them to cling to.

"May I see your bedroom?" she asked.

"There isn't much to see, but if it matters—"

"It does," she cut in quickly.

He pointed the way, and when they walked into his room, he saw that he'd forgotten to make his bed that morning. The top sheet was pulled back, the quilt bunched into a navy blue heap.

She studied the jumbled bedding, then turned to take inventory of the items cluttering the accessory caddy on his dresser. He knew the instant she'd spotted the condoms. The foil packets weren't hard to miss.

"Safe sex," he said.

"With whom?" she asked, her voice a little shaky.

"No one." He snuffed out his cigarette, making use of the ashtray on his nightstand. "Not for a while."

"Me, neither. Not since David. I didn't enter WIT-SEC looking for a lover." She exhaled an audible breath. "I stayed on the Pill because it keeps me on a twenty-eight-day cycle."

Great, he thought. They'd gone from condoms to the Pill to the frequency of her menstrual flow.

"Would you like something to drink?" he asked, changing the subject a bit too abruptly.

She blinked and nodded, accepting his awkward

hospitality. "I'm sorry. I didn't mean to make you uncomfortable."

"No harm done." As he escorted her from his room, he breathed in the fragrance of her hair, the soft, airy scent he remembered all too well.

Once they were seated on his sofa with cans of soda in front of them, she glanced around and noticed the leather-bound photo album on a side table.

"May I?" she asked.

"Sure. Go ahead. My mom put it together a long time ago." He removed his jacket and unholstered his gun, preparing to settle into the moment, to share bits and pieces of his life with the lady he'd vowed to protect.

With Juliet, he thought uncomfortably. With the Capulet he wasn't supposed to want.

Nine

"**O**h, my goodness. Is this you?" Natalie gazed at a photograph of a little boy with dark bangs and an impish smile.

Zack shifted beside her. "I was four years old."

"Look at your clothes." She couldn't hide her smile. He wore a turtleneck sweater and plaid pants, with a wide belt cinched at his waist.

"What can I say? It was the sixties." He leaned into her, his arm brushing hers. "Check this out. That's my mom. I never could figure out what that bubble on top of her head was."

"That's her hair." Natalie bumped Zack's shoulder, and they both laughed. A moment later, she studied the picture more closely. The young woman in the snapshot was slim, with subdued makeup and a modest flip, despite the bubble. A military wife, Natalie thought, with a pretty blue dress and white shoes. "What's her name?"

"Donna."

"She's lovely." Natalie tried to imagine Donna now, but it was difficult to envisage her with Alzheimer's. "Is her dementia bad?"

"It was the last time I visited her. Some days are worse than others." He turned the page. "That's my father. His name was Dean."

Natalie's heart struck her chest. She could see Zack's resemblance to Dean Ryder—the dark deep-set eyes, hollowed cheekbones, strong jaw. Dean's hair was buzzed, a reflection of the soldier he'd been. She glanced at the next photograph, a five-by-seven portrait that presented both of Zack's parents. Donna was pregnant, and Dean wore the expression of a proud, soon-to-be father. "They look happy."

"My white grandparents weren't too thrilled. Interracial marriages weren't very common in those days, and they were worried about what other people would say." Zack touched the edge of the picture, skimming the yellowed corners. "And to top it off, my dad's family was poor. Really poor. They had no electricity, no heating system, no plumbing. Just a shack with an outhouse." He paused, his voice tinged with sadness. "Poverty, alcoholism, children being forced into mission schools. That was typical of the reservation at that time. It's still bad."

Natalie knew what it was like to be poor—city poor.

But she realized that wasn't the same. "Did he have a big family?"

"He had an older sister and a bunch of cousins." Zack reached for his soda and took a sip. "Everybody lived together, but aside from an aging grandfather, it was mostly women and children. The younger men didn't stick around."

Like my dad, Natalie thought. She gazed at Dean's image and wondered if he'd missed having a father.

Zack replaced his drink. "It's strange that my mom took a chance on an Indian guy. She wasn't exactly a society girl, but she was raised in an upper-middle-class neighborhood. I think that's why she didn't stay in touch with my dad's family after he died. She didn't know how to relate to them. They didn't have a TV, a radio or a phone. She couldn't call them and chat about everyday things. They were isolated from her world."

"And now you're isolated from theirs." Natalie looked into his eyes. She wanted to touch him, to trace the features he'd inherited from his Sioux ancestors, but she kept her hands on the photo album instead.

"I don't blame my mom for that," he said. "She tried to keep my dad's memory alive."

"What sorts of things did she tell you about him?"

"That he appreciated city living. That he had a good heart and a dry sense of humor." Zack chuckled. "That he used to wake up every morning and thank the Creator for pizza, popcorn and toilets that flushed."

Natalie glanced at Dean's picture, charmed by his

smile, by the man Donna had fallen in love with. "Did he talk about his heritage?"

"Not much. According to my mom, he went to a mission school and practiced Christianity. But he was proud of the warriors from his Nation. I think he enlisted in the navy to prove what kind of Lakota he was. To become a warrior."

After a bout of silence, he leaned into her again, turning another page in the photo album. She could smell his cologne, a blend of wood smoke and spice, of forest-green days and dark, exotic nights.

"This is Uncle Joe," he said.

Distracted, she struggled to focus. A second later her gaze landed on a picture of a brown-haired man, with blue eyes and a powerful presence. "The deputy U.S. marshal? The one who died over a decade ago?"

"That's him. My mom's older brother."

"You look a little bit like him." Same aura, she thought. Same commanding vibe.

"He helped raise me. He became my father figure."

"And you followed in his footsteps."

"Yes." Zack's dark eyebrows drew together, forming a frown. "He influenced every aspect of my life."

She examined his troubled expression. "Was your uncle hard to please?"

He shook his head. "No. He was a good man. He would do just about anything for me. I was the son he never had."

"Then what is it?" she asked. "What's wrong?"

"Uncle Joe was at the siege at Wounded Knee."

Natalie blinked back her surprise. "He exchanged

gunfire with the Indians? He was one of the marshals battling your father's people?''

''Uncle Joe didn't think of them as my father's people. He didn't think my dad would have supported the group who occupied Wounded Knee.''

''And what did you think?''

Zack closed the photo album, shutting out the pictures, blocking his childhood. ''I was too young to understand what was going on, to see beyond what I was told.''

''And later?'' she asked.

''I ignored the truth. I chalked it up to the past, told myself it didn't matter.''

Natalie watched memories flicker across his eyes. Faded images, she thought. Shattered dreams. ''But it did, didn't it?''

''Yes,'' he agreed. ''It mattered. The Indians at Wounded Knee were fighting for the Sioux, for their rights. At the time, the tribal president at Pine Ridge was corrupt. He abolished freedom of speech and assembly on the reservation. He misused funds.'' Zack paused to finish his soda, to frown at the can. ''The Indians who occupied Wounded Knee were making a stand. And why the hell not? The reservation was practically a war zone. Opponents of the tribal president's regime were being beaten and shot.''

Natalie searched her memory, trying to recall the movie she'd seen about the siege. ''There were racial problems, too.''

He nodded. ''Lots of tension. The border towns were riddled with prejudice. Prior to the siege, a white man had stabbed a young Indian man to death, and a fight broke out at the trial. The victim's mother spent several weeks in jail, but her son's killer was acquitted without doing time.''

When he fell silent, she touched his hand. He curled his fingers around hers and exhaled a deep breath. ''It makes me feel like a traitor. Uncle Joe was at Wounded Knee, and he was my mentor, a man I loved and admired.''

''He was doing his job, what he thought was right.''

''I know, but is that what I'm supposed to say to my Lakota relatives?''

''You're not the enemy, Zack. You're family.''

He didn't respond. He left the couch and walked toward the fireplace. Natalie assumed he was going to retrieve something from the mantel, but he veered to the left, where a cedar chest sat. Sunlight spilled in from the window, sending gilded patterns over the aging wood. He kneeled to open the chest and came back to her carrying a folded quilt. When he placed it on her lap, she touched the fabric and looked up at him.

''It belonged to my father. His mother made it for him when he enlisted in the navy. Star quilts are often given to Lakota children throughout their lives.'' He unfolded a portion of the fabric, revealing the colorful design. ''It's a way to honor them.''

''It's beautiful.'' And she could see how much it meant to him, realizing it was probably the only tangible connection he could claim.

''Some families adorn a loved one's casket with a quilt, but my father had a military burial.'' He traced a point on the star. "Quilting was introduced to the Plains tribes from missionaries in the nineteenth and early twentieth centuries. Native girls in boarding schools were taught to make quilts, and now the star design is synonymous with Indian country." His voice shifted, his tone quiet. "On the day my mom found out that my dad died, she slept with this." He paused to smooth the material, to refold the edges. "I remember her curling up with it, cradling it against her body, mourning him."

Natalie met his gaze, tempted to hold him, to make the pain go away. "I'm sorry," she said.

Zack blew a rough breath. "I was young and my memories are vague, but I'll never forget the way she cried. I didn't understand death, not completely, but I knew that my daddy wasn't coming home, that we'd never see him again."

Silent, she handed him the quilt, and he returned it to the cedar chest. Natalie wasn't close to her family, but she could relate to his loss. She knew how it felt to be alone, to wish for comfort that wasn't there.

And now his job was on the line, too.

"I'm sorry," she said again.

He stood in front of the fireplace, the brick-and-stone structure at his back. "Me, too."

She looked around. His living room was decorated in earth tones, with wood furniture and rugged accessories. A cluttered bookcase held paperbacks, leather volumes and an ancient set of encyclopedias. A sliding-glass door led to a spacious yard flourishing with trees. Did he spend his mornings there? Sipping coffee, smoking cigarettes and listening to birds sing?

When her breath clogged her lungs, she touched a hand to her heart. Her Zack, she thought. "I'm going to miss you."

He dragged his fingers through his hair, spiking the thick, dark strands, looking like a lone warrior on a troubled day. "We're an unlikely pair." He smiled a little, the corners of his mouth titling in an offbeat way. "Who would've guessed?"

"No kidding." She smiled, too. "The mistress and the marshal." She knew they weren't meant to be, but for now, she wanted to keep him close, to hold on to him for as long as she could.

Two days later, Zack knocked on Natalie's door, armed with information about the psychiatrist WIT-SEC arranged for her to see. She answered the summons, and his mind went blank. Long-limbed and barefoot, she wore a flowing summer dress, with an unexpected accessory—a platinum-haired toddler attached to her hip.

The kid made a shy face and tugged on the neckline of her dress, stretching buttonholes. Just as Zack got a glimpse of her bra, another little head popped out from behind the folds of her skirt.

"I'm baby-sitting," she said.

Still stuck on her bra—pink lace and cream-colored satin—it took him a moment to realize they were her landlord's children.

Brice, the older one, grabbed his pant leg. "Remember me? I'm the bad-guy Martian. Can I see your badge?''

Forcing his brain to kick into gear, Zack kneeled to accommodate the boy, recalling the youngster's interest in his profession at the barbecue. Not that the kid knew the difference between a deputy marshal and a highway patrolman, but he flashed the shield. To a five-year-old, a cop was a cop.

''Wow.'' Brice stared at the badge as if it were studded with diamonds.

Zack remained silent. What could he say, knowing he'd defiled it? He glanced up and caught Natalie watching him. Self-conscious, he ruffled Brice's hair and got to his feet.

''Would you like to come in?'' she asked. ''We were just about to make some lunch.''

Before he could respond, Brice chimed in. ''Will ya, Officer Zack?''

''Sure. But it's Deputy Zack.''

The foursome entered the kitchen, with Timmy, the two-year-old, still clinging to Natalie, still giving Zack a peep show. Trying to ignore the bits of lace between her buttons, he wiggled the child's foot and got a leave-me-alone whine in return.

''He misses his mommy,'' she said.

''And you're the next best thing?'' Not that he could blame the boy. Then again, she did look a tad weary around the edges. ''How did you end up babysitting?''

''Their regular sitter came down with the flu, and

Carla had an appointment this afternoon she couldn't miss.''

"My brother won't let go of Natalie," Brice offered, nosing into the adult conversation. "He screams if she tries to put him down. Real loud. And he won't take a nap, neither.''

"How long have you been holding him?" Zack asked.

She peered at the microwave clock. "Almost three hours.''

Damn. No wonder she looked so weary. Her arms were probably aching by now. "Maybe I can help.'' Not that he was an expert where toddlers were concerned, but he was willing to try. He looked around for something to amuse the boy, came up with a paper plate and started a game of peekaboo, making as many goofy faces as he could master.

Timmy studied him, somber at first. But after a few swishes of the plate, he grinned and giggled.

"You're easy." Zack poked the child's belly and got another laugh. Natalie laughed, too, and he had the urge to hug her.

He reached out to Timmy instead.

The two-year-old latched on to Natalie's dress like a sailor bracing for a storm.

Guilty, Zack watched her cradle the boy, her arms straining. "Maybe we can dance. All four of us. Then we can switch partners." He shifted his attention to the older child, hoping for a little Martian support. "Sound okay to you?''

"Yeah!" Brice agreed and Zack scooped him up, ready for the next phase.

"How about you?" he asked Natalie.

"I'm game," she said.

"Then let's do it." Zack moved forward and closed the circle, balancing Brice in one arm and putting his other arm around Natalie. She looked into his eyes, smiled, made his heart go weak.

"Ready?" He rocked everyone to a humming beat, then quickened the pace, twirling his companions like a human carousel. Brice joined in with a kindergarten song, and Timmy gulped and giggled.

They switched partners without a hitch, exchanging kids. Before Timmy noticed who was holding him, Zack gave him a noisy raspberry, blowing on his chubby little arm. Somewhere in the back of his mind, Natalie's perfume scented the air. It was a heady combination, he thought. A beautiful woman and two healthy happy children.

She whispered, "Thank you," in his ear and ended the dance, setting the older, heavier child back on his feet. Zack kept Timmy in his arms, rubbing his cheek against the boy's hair, wondering how fatherhood had passed him by.

Natalie made lunch, doling out peanut-butter-and-jelly sandwiches, with canned pears and crackers on the side.

"This came from our house," Brice announced, pointing to the peanut butter. "It's our favorite kind."

Ignoring Timmy's highchair, Zack took a seat at the table, bouncing the contented youngster on his lap. He hadn't eaten a peanut-butter-and-jelly sandwich since he was a kid. He took a bite, chewed, felt the bread stick to the roof of his mouth. "Tastes the same."

Natalie sat across from him. "As what?"

"As the way my mom used to make them."

"That good, huh?"

"Yeah." They smiled at each other and he wished she wasn't the woman who'd damaged his career, who'd inspired him to break every rule he'd vowed to uphold.

Timmy grabbed a handful of crackers from Zack's plate, and he stopped the boy from cramming them into his mouth. "Hold on, buddy." He reached for the sandwich Natalie had fixed for the two-year-old. "Try this first. It's cut up all nice and neat for you."

Timmy took the offering, then filled his cheeks like a chipmunk. All too soon, his hands turned gooey, sticky with food-encrusted saliva. A glob of squished-up something-or-other landed on his shirt.

Natalie cocked her head. "I guess I should have put a bib on him." When the boy clapped and sent bits of moist bread flying, she hopped out of her chair. "Oh, Timmy, honey. You're making a mess."

She reached for the child, and Zack breathed a guilty sigh of relief. So much for the fatherhood-passed-him-by thing.

Within no time, she had the little one settled into a highchair, hands and face washed, a cartoon-printed bib in place. Upon contact, Timmy started squishing his food again. Refusing to be upstaged, Brice spilled his milk.

Zack and Natalie looked at each other. He wasn't sure who laughed first. Brice laughed, too, and Timmy squealed in piggy-face delight.

Finally, Natalie rose to clean up the milk. Using a kitchen towel, she went to work. Zack kneeled to help her, catching the overflow with a wad of napkins.

Brice swung his foot and kicked Zack in the head. Natalie, her eyes shining, bit back another bout of laughter. He barely noticed the kid's grungy shoe. Suddenly he didn't want the day to end, to let Natalie go. He wanted to make a few more memories, to stretch their friendship just a little further.

"Have dinner with me tonight," he said. "Let me take you out."

Still sopping up the mess, she grabbed Brice's foot before he nailed Zack again. And then she accepted his invitation with a sweet, girlish smile.

Natalie tried to tell herself this wasn't a date, but the romantic ambience fooled her senses. The restaurant overlooked the lake, with moonbeams dancing on the water. Zack sat across from her at their table, a cozy wooden booth decorated with candlelight and a long-stemmed rose.

"You look beautiful," he said.

"Thank you." She'd labored over her appearance, choosing a slim red dress and heels. "You look good, too." Good enough to kiss, she thought. His smile warmed the night, and soft-hued shadows edged his face.

He reached for his wine, and Natalie sampled the

appetizers: eggplant bruschetta and lobster-and-crab-stuffed mushrooms. She couldn't remember the last time she'd dined in a quiet restaurant, with stars in her eyes.

"I promise we'll find you a car this week." He glanced at a passing waiter. "It shouldn't have taken this long."

"We've had a lot going on." An affair that had changed their lives, a moment in time that made her ache. She could still feel his touch—his mouth, his hands, the power of his body spilling into hers.

Zack tasted his salad, and she watched him eat, trying to imagine the months passing without him. Fall days, winter nights, next spring.

"Will you take me to my appointment on Thursday?" she asked.

"You know I will." His gaze caught hers. "Are you nervous?"

She nodded. The idea of talking to a psychiatrist, of discussing her nightmares out loud wasn't something she wanted to face. "Is there any way I can get out of this?"

"Not if I can help it." He slid his hand across the table and took hers. "But it's going to be okay. You'll do fine."

She locked her fingers through his, holding on to him like a lifeline. "Does the doctor know who I am?"

"She knows you're in the program."

"Is she nice?"

His lips tilted in an amused smile. "Would I send you to someone mean?"

Natalie managed a relieved laugh. "No, I suppose not." She realized this wasn't the proper setting to continue this conversation, to ask him details about a WITSEC-approved psychiatrist.

Fifteen minutes later, their entrées arrived. He'd ordered slow-roasted salmon and she'd chosen a seafood pasta dish.

"I mentioned you to my mom," he said.

Surprised, she lifted her fork. "You did?"

"Sort of. She doesn't understand what's going on in my life. She thinks I work at the nursing home where she lives." He cut into the salmon. "But that could change. Next time she might think I'm George Clooney."

Natalie blinked. "The actor?"

"She watches a lot of TV. Old reruns of *ER*." In typical Zack fashion, he grinned. "I've got that Clooney vibe, don't you think?"

Charmed, she raised her eyebrows at him. "Dream on, Deputy."

"Says the lady who can't resist me."

Her heart bumped her chest. Were they flirting? Pretending that they hadn't complicated each other's lives? "Who does your mom think I am?"

He drained his wine, lingered over the glass. The flame on the candle flickered, swaying like a lone dancer. "Juliet."

"Shakespeare's Juliet?"

He nodded. "It's silly, isn't it?"

Silly? She gazed at the wax pooling over the side of the candle, then looked up to see Zack watching her. Sights and sounds from the restaurant disappeared, intensifying her pulse, the vein fluttering at her wrist, the blood flowing through her body. "What did you tell your mother about me?"

"She asked if I had a girlfriend, and I said there was someone I wasn't supposed to be with." His voice turned low, a little rough, like sandpaper in the dark. "It was as close to the truth as I could manage."

The truth. Natalie drew a breath, trapped within the beat of her heart. The flame was still dancing, the wax still melting. She could almost feel it dripping over her skin, encasing her in warmth. In Zack's embrace. In the man she was sure to lose.

"Are you all right?" he asked.

No, she thought. She would never be all right again. Because at that moment, at that very instant, she knew what was happening.

Juliet was falling in love.

Ten

After dinner, Natalie and Zack walked along a street that showcased the lake. Although the evening air was cool, Natalie welcomed the water-scented breeze. She allowed it to caress her face, to tousle her hair, to wrap itself around her emotions.

She'd fallen in love with her field inspector, with the deputy marshal assigned to protect her.

"Are you cold?" he asked.

She turned to look at him. Moonlight shimmered in his eyes, and the wind rustled his clothes. He wore a dark gray suit and a black tie. His shoulders were broad and strong, and she imagined leaning into him, kissing him, telling him that she loved him. But she knew she couldn't. Things were complicated enough.

"It's a little chilly, but I don't mind. I like being out-side."

"How about a hot drink? There's a gourmet coffee bar up ahead."

"Sounds good."

They walked in silence, side by side, without touching. Ten minutes later, they sat on a lone bench that faced the water, sipping mocha-flavored cappuccinos. Zack's drink was decaffeinated, but Natalie remained true to her addiction, to her nightly boost of caffeine. She tasted the whipped cream on top, then licked her lips, savoring the sweetness.

Zack shifted beside her. "I'm confused."

"About what?"

"My job." He paused to sip his coffee, to meet her gaze. "Maybe I should turn in my resignation."

"And give up your badge?"

"I might lose it anyway."

"But what if you don't? What if they allow you to keep it? I realize you wouldn't be part of WITSEC anymore, but you'd still be a deputy."

The wind whipped his hair back. "I know, but after everything that's happened, it might be better to start over."

Her heart skipped an anxious beat. She couldn't help but think about the inspector who'd quit his job to marry a witness. "Start over?"

He nodded. "With a new career. I'm more than qualified to work as a security consultant. To open my own firm."

"In Spokane?" She scooted closer, her imagination

soaring. If he resigned from the Marshal Service, he would be free to be with her, to remain part of her life. Of course, if he were fired, he would be free as well, but that wouldn't be the same. "Maybe you could open a company in Coeur d'Alene?" She gave him a hopeful smile. "We'd both have businesses here. After I start school, I'm going to focus on my boutique."

He skimmed her cheek, running the pad of his thumb along her skin. It was a touch she'd come to know, a touch she craved. "I wouldn't stay in this area, Natalie."

"Where would you go?" she asked, as he dropped his hand.

"I'm not sure. Maybe back to Illinois."

She glanced at the water. Suddenly it seemed ominous. Lonely. "What about your mom?"

"I'd bring her with me. I'd find a good nursing home for her there. Besides, that's where she met my dad, where she raised me."

"You sound as if you're going to do this, Zack."

"I don't know." He sighed. "Maybe I am."

"Would you be willing to keep in touch with me? To call once in a while?" She gazed into his eyes and prayed for a positive response. Something, anything that would keep them connected.

"I don't think that's a good idea." He smoothed a strand of hair from her forehead, a touch too fleeting for her to claim. "It would be easier if we moved on, if we didn't look back."

She gripped her coffee, pressing the paper cup to

her chest. Zack wanted to start a new life without her, she thought. To exclude her from his future.

And why not? She was the woman who'd tainted his badge, who'd jeopardized his WITSEC career, who'd forced him to reevaluate his life.

"I understand," she said.

"No matter what I decide, I won't do anything until you're ready to deal with a new inspector." He kept his voice low, gentle. "I'll wait until you get the chance to work through your nightmares. To get the help you need."

I need you, she thought. She needed her protector.

An elderly couple approached, then stopped to gaze at the lake. Both Zack and Natalie fell silent.

The husband slipped his arm around his wife. In turn, she leaned her head on his shoulder, peaceful in his embrace.

Natalie couldn't help but wonder how long they'd been married, how many children they'd raised, how many grandchildren they boasted about.

But most of all, she wondered how it would feel to grow old with someone. With Zack, she thought. With the man she loved.

On Thursday morning Zack had already taken Natalie to the psychiatrist and now they were seated in her living room, eating breakfast sandwiches from a fast-food joint. Natalie picked at her ham and cheese biscuit, taking small bites. She hadn't said a word about the hour-long session, but she'd booked another appointment for next week.

She didn't look well. Her skin was pale and shadows plagued her eyes. Zack sipped his orange juice, wondering if he should question her. In the old days, an inspector used to handle every aspect of a witness's life, even psychological dilemmas. Sending someone to a psychiatrist hadn't been part of the program.

Times had changed, he thought. But witnesses still struggled. Natalie occupied a chair across from the sofa, lost in thought.

"Are you all right?" he asked.

She glanced up from her sandwich. "I didn't do it."

"You didn't tell the doctor about your nightmares?"

She twisted the napkin in her lap. "Not completely. I didn't want to give her details about the murder."

"But you told the police. The feds. The prosecutors."

"No, I didn't. Not all of it."

Zack merely nodded. It wasn't unusual for witnesses to withhold information, things they could use as a bargaining tool if they got into trouble later. But Natalie wasn't a criminal wheeling and dealing for government perks. Her reluctance went much deeper. "You can tell her next time."

"Maybe I can practice on you first." She set her sandwich on the coffee table. "Do you think that would be okay?"

"Of course it is." He realized she was building the courage to earn her doctor's trust. In spite of the psychiatrist's medical degree, the other woman was a stranger to Natalie. And Zack, the deputy marshal she'd slept with, qualified as a friend. "You can tell me anything."

"I have nightmares about what David did to me on the day of the murder." She drew her legs up, curling into the chair, into herself. "I planned a weekend getaway. David had a vacation home in the country, and I asked him to take me there. To spend some quality time together." She fidgeted with the straw in her orange juice. "It was a big place, surrounded by a forested area."

Zack knew where the murder had occurred, but he realized Natalie needed to start from the beginning.

"On the first day we were there, one of his associates showed up," she said. "A man named Kevin Peters. It was obvious David had asked him to come by, to work through a deal."

"Drug trafficking?"

"Yes. But I didn't know that at the time. I wasn't involved in David's business." She sipped her drink, wetting her mouth. Her voice had gone raspy. "I was hurt that David had interrupted our weekend, but I was trying to make the best of it. While the men were in the den, speaking privately, I was in the kitchen, making David's favorite snack. Double-fudge brownies. We were supposed to have a picnic later."

Zack watched her, waiting for her to explain further. He could see the fear in her eyes, the memories creeping into her mind.

"The men started arguing, snapping at each other. I could hear them raising their voices. But I stayed out of it. It wasn't my place to interfere."

"So you kept making the brownies?"

"Yes. I was getting ready to put them in the oven." She paused, took a breath. "Then suddenly there was a loud noise. A blast. I knew it was a gunshot. I dropped the pan and tore off running. I thought Kevin had shot David."

"But that isn't what happened."

"No. It was David who'd fired the gun." She gripped her drink, her hands trembling. "Kevin was lying on the floor, and there was...there was blood and gunk everywhere. David had shot him in the back of the head, at close range. He'd blown half of his brains out."

Zack knew that Halloway had killed his associate when the other man had turned away, attempting to leave.

"David started screaming, saying that Kevin was cheating him. That he'd reneged on their deal. I just stood there, like a zombie. I couldn't move. I couldn't talk. I couldn't think."

When her voice broke, he held out his hand, inviting her to sit beside him on the sofa, to come closer. She accepted his offer, and he knew she needed the comfort of human contact. He touched her knee, and her breath hitched.

"You don't have to tell me the rest," he said. "Not if you can't handle it."

"I'm already halfway there." What good would it do to stop now? Natalie thought. It wouldn't block her nightmares. It wouldn't change anything. "I backed away from Kevin's body. I told David that he had to call the police. That he had to admit that he'd killed Kevin in a fit of anger. That he hadn't meant to do it.'' She gazed at Zack, at his somber expression. ''But David wouldn't listen. He said he was going to dispose of the body and that I was going to help him. He claimed we were in this together.''

''And what did you say to him?''

''I told him that I couldn't do it. That no matter how much I loved him, I wouldn't be an accessory to murder. And that's when he lunged at me. When he held the gun to my head.''

Zack's voice turned hard. ''That son of a bitch.''

''He called me a stupid whore. He said I was nothing to him. Nothing but a Barbie doll he could break in two.'' She could still hear those ugly words, still see the truth in her lover's eyes. ''He'd never loved me. I was just a toy, a woman who catered to his every whim.''

''A teenage girl he'd made into a mistress.''

''Yes.'' And that hurt most of all. She'd been naive enough to think that being his mistress counted, that it made her important, that someday he would leave his wife for her. ''The gun was a single-action revolver, one of David's other toys. He always kept loaded weapons around.''

''How long did he hold it to your head?''

''I don't know. Several minutes, I guess. It seemed like hours.'' Natalie exhaled a shaky breath, recalling the fear, the humiliation of being tortured by a man she'd loved. ''I kept saying, 'David don't do this.' But he was beyond reason. He told me that we were going to play a game. That fate would decide if I lived or died.''

''Russian roulette?''

She nodded. ''That's what I have nightmares about. David leaving one bullet in the chamber, spinning the cylinder, cocking the hammer.'' The weakness in her knees as he pulled the trigger, as she waited for her head to explode. ''Afterward, he said, 'You won. You get to live. Now help me clean up this mess.' So that's what I did. I was in shock, but I helped him wipe up the blood and scrape Kevin's brains off the wall. I have nightmares about that, too.''

''I'm so sorry.'' Zack reached for her and she fell into his embrace.

As he stroked her hair, she clung to him. His heart was beating against hers, and she welcomed the steady rhythm, the warmth of being near him. ''While we were scrubbing the floor, David apologized to me. I just looked at him and burst into tears. He hugged me. He actually put his arms around me, thinking I would forgive him.''

Zack pressed his lips to her temple, and she wished he were the man she'd loved all those years. That he had been her lover instead of David. ''After we cleaned up the mess, David went to work on the gun, grinding off the serial number and altering the barrel, the chamber and anything else that could identify the murder weapon.'' She paused to inhale the scent of Zack's skin, his woodsy cologne, the hint of tobacco. ''David had already wrapped a trash bag around Kevin's head to stop the blood from dripping, and we were supposed to bury the body that night. But when David went into the bathroom to take a shower, I called the police. I turned him in.''

''Why didn't you tell the police that Halloway had attempted to kill you? That he'd held a gun to your head.''

She closed her eyes, then opened them a moment later, trapped within her shame. ''Because I didn't want the police or the FBI or the prosecutors to know that David thought so little of me. That he didn't value me the way he valued his wife.'' She pulled back to catch her breath. ''Ironic, isn't it? Since David's wife is determined to see me dead.''

He cupped her face. ''That isn't going to happen. WITSEC doesn't lose witnesses, Natalie. As long as you remain in the program, you'll be safe.''

But I won't have you, she thought, as she met his gaze. She wouldn't have Zack.

Later that night, Zack stepped out of the shower and grabbed a towel. He'd left Natalie's house hours ago, but couldn't stop thinking about her.

Squinting through the steam, he wiped off the mirror, then frowned at his reflection. Sooner or later, he and Natalie would part ways. And deep down, he knew that was the best thing for both of them. But that didn't make him miss her any less. Nor did it keep him from worrying about her.

Should he call her? Make sure she was okay? She'd found the strength to tell him about her nightmares, but that didn't mean she wouldn't be afraid to fall asleep tonight.

Zack wrapped the towel around his waist and headed for the phone. He dialed her number and waited. When she didn't answer, he glanced at the clock. Why hadn't she picked up by now? She couldn't be asleep already. Not at 10 p.m.

Finally, she came on the line, her voice breathless.

He gripped the receiver. "Where were you? What took you so long?"

"Zack?" She paused for a moment. "I was in the tub. I had to jump out to grab the phone."

She was naked? Dripping water all over the floor? He tried to think of something else, to block his imagination, but he pictured her anyway. Creamy skin, lean curves, moisture trailing between her thighs.

"I'm in a towel," he said stupidly.

"You are?"

"Yeah." He cleared his throat, told himself this wasn't the time to get aroused. "I just took a shower."

"Really?" She made a soft sound. "I filled the tub with bath oil, with those little beads that dissolve in the water. I love that feeling."

"I've never used bath oil."

She laughed a little. "I guess it's a girl thing."

He sat on the edge of the bed and readjusted his towel. His body wasn't obeying his mind. And to make matters worse, he had the urge to lie down, to close his eyes, to listen to her voice and—

"Why did you call?" she asked.

His mind went blank, as empty as a chalkboard at

the end of a teacher's day. Suddenly he couldn't remember why he'd dialed her number.

"Zack?" she pressed.

"What?"

"Are you all right?"

He shifted his legs, glanced at the condoms on his dresser, wondered what she would say if he told her he wanted to make love to her, just one more time. "I'm fine."

"I'm getting cold."

His brain snapped into focus. "I'm sorry. Do you want to put the phone down and get your robe?"

"I already grabbed a sheet."

And the bath-oil beads were melting without her, he thought. "I just wanted to make sure you were okay. That you weren't afraid to go to sleep tonight."

"The doctor gave me some pills. These little sample packets." She paused. "But I'd rather drink some coffee and stay up."

He turned down the light. "Don't do that, baby. Don't force yourself to stay awake."

"I wish you were here, Zack."

"I know. But I'm just a phone call away if you need me. And we'll see each other soon. We'll shop for your car."

"A Pinto?" she asked and made him laugh.

"As long as we're talking horses." He shifted the receiver and imagined holding her, drawing her into his arms. "How about a Mustang? Maybe a convertible." Something sporty, he thought. Something that would match the little red dress she'd worn the other night.

"That sounds perfect. Why didn't we think of that before?"

"I don't know. Are you still cold?"

"Not as much." Her voice dropped off for a second and he wondered if her sheet had slipped. "You're keeping me warm," she said.

"Me, too." He gave up and climbed into bed. What man wouldn't get warm?

"Are you still wearing a towel?" she asked.

He glanced at the terry cloth wrapped around his waist. "Yes." But they shouldn't be having this conversation. Not while his room was dim and moonlight slashed through the blinds. Not while he was half-naked and wanting her. "You better finish your bath and get some sleep."

"Are you going to go to sleep, too?"

"I'm going to try."

"Thank you, Zack."

"For what?"

"For calling." Her breath rushed out. "For caring."

"You're welcome," he said, wishing caring didn't hurt so much. "'Night, Natalie."

"Good night," she whispered, as he waited for her to hang up, to end the connection, to leave him much too alone.

Eleven

Zack tossed and turned. He'd shut off the light and tried to sleep, but Natalie remained on his mind. He rolled over and smacked his hand against the headboard, scraping his knuckles. He'd discarded the towel, only to battle his nakedness. The top sheet slid along his skin, making him more aroused, more frustrated.

Maybe he should give up the fight. Release the tension. Stroke himself into a hand-pumping daze.

And make a sticky mess all over his bed? He kicked away the blanket and laughed, cursed, shoved his pillow between his legs.

The telephone rang and he shot up like a rocket and fumbled for the receiver, nearly knocking it onto the floor.

"Natalie?"

"How did you know it was me?"

"I didn't." Zack flipped on the light. Her name had been a reflex, a pulse-jarring instinct, a flash of masculine heat. An hour had passed since he'd heard her voice, since they'd said good-night. "What's going on?"

"I can't sleep."

He sat up, his pillow still jammed between his legs, pressing the hardness. "Me, neither."

"I didn't take those pills, but I didn't drink any coffee, either. I've just been lying here. I can't stop thinking about you, Zack."

He closed his eyes, felt his body react. "Did you finish your bath?"

"Mmm. But I had to refill the tub. Warm up the water."

Her voice turned soft, and he envisaged her in her room, dressed in a filmy nightgown, curled up with the comforter. Eyelet and lace, he thought. Sexual surrender.

He opened his eyes, pushed away the pillow. "Can I come over?"

"To sleep on the couch?"

He drew his knees up, shifted his legs, let the air stimulate his skin. "No."

Her breath hitched. "To touch me?"

"Yes." To put his hands all over her. To keep breaking rules. To curse himself into oblivion when it was done. "Just one more time."

"Can I touch you?" she asked. "Can I use my mouth?"

He wet his lips, swallowed his own saliva, felt his pulse quicken. "I'll die if you don't." Maybe he was dying now. She lived over an hour away.

"I'll wait for you," she said.

"Then I'll be there," he told her. "As soon as I can."

Too aroused to think straight, he hung up the phone and stumbled into his jeans, then realized he'd forgotten underwear. Since he wasn't about to backtrack, he worked the zipper over his turgid flesh, left the snap undone and pulled a T-shirt over his head. Finally, he shoved his feet into a pair of socks, grabbed lace-up boots and fumbled with the ties. On his way out the door, he snagged the overnight bag he always kept packed.

Once he was inside the car, he lit a cigarette, turned on the radio and fought the urge to speed. He wasn't on duty. Rushing off to have sex with a female witness didn't qualify as a security assignment.

He shook his head and blew a stream of smoke into the air. Zack Ryder, he thought. The deputy from hell.

By the time he arrived at Natalie's house, his conscience racked his brain. He pulled into her driveway and killed the engine. How could he keep doing this? How could he keep cheating his job?

When she answered the door, he knew why. He stepped inside, and they stared at each other. She wore a nightgown similar to the one he'd imagined. The twilight-colored fabric clung to her curves, shimmering to the ground in a stream of silk. She was naked underneath. He could see the outline of her breasts, the shadow between her thighs.

"Hi," she said.

"Hi." He repeated her greeting and leaned into her. She put her arms around him and he held her. She smelled like citrus and cream, like lemons dipped in sugar. "Did you mean what you said on the phone?"

"About what?"

He pulled her closer and cupped her bottom, rubbing her against his fly. She made a soft, achy sound, and he knew her legs had gone weak, that he'd made her wet. "About using your mouth?"

She clung to his waist. "Yes."

He nuzzled her neck, nipped her scented skin. "I want to taste you, too."

"We'll take turns." She brushed her mouth over his, teasing him, making his blood swim. "But I want to go first. I want to make you crazy."

He stepped back to look at her, to feed the fantasy. Her lips were glossed with a pale pink color, full and lush. "Then do it." He removed his shirt and unzipped his jeans, inviting her to drop to her knees. "Make me crazy."

She moved forward, and his heart pole-vaulted to his throat. When she touched him, it was a feathery motion, the tips of her fingers against his stomach.

A temptation. The flutter of a sin.

Finally, she kneeled to kiss his navel, branding him, making him yearn for her tongue, for the pleasure he craved. As she opened his pants even more, he watched her, anticipating what came next.

"Zack." She said his name before she licked the tip of his arousal, seducing him with warmth, with slow, gentle moisture.

He didn't close his eyes. He couldn't. His gaze was riveted to her, to what she was doing. When she looked up at him, he knew he was lost. Sweet, sensual Natalie. She knew how to satisfy the craving.

She used that luscious mouth, and he shifted his stance and rolled his hips, rocking into the rhythm, encouraging her to take him as deeply as she could. He caressed her face while she did it. He even ran his fingers over her lips, tracing the shape, touching her while she licked and sucked and drove him mad.

His heartbeat blasted his chest; his pulse pounded between his legs. He could barely think, barely reason. Somewhere in the back of his mind, he realized they were still in the entryway of her house.

For a moment, for one dizzy instant, he feared the power she wielded over him. Oral sex. The pressure of her mouth, the swirl of her tongue. He couldn't get enough.

"Natalie." He combed his fingers through her hair, tousling the golden strands. She looked like a jungle nymph, with her cat eyes and long, lean body. She pushed his jeans down even more, then rubbed her face all over him, against his arousal, against his thighs.

"I'm not going to make it," he said. He was too turned on, too excited, too desperate to come.

She pulled back, just a little, just enough to stroke him with her hands, to bring him to an earth-shattering climax. He spilled against the front of her nightgown, soaking the material with his seed.

She came to her feet and peeled the garment from her body, letting it drop to the floor. Zack reached for her, holding her tight against him. Her heartbeat pounded in time with his. Erratic, he thought. So damn shaky.

It was easy to get addicted to her, to that warm, willing mouth. But it was easy to put his mouth all over her, too. He slid his fingers down her spine and inhaled the flavor of her skin. Lemons. Cream. Sugar. He wanted to eat her alive.

She kissed him, a light, sweet kiss—gentler than he could have imagined.

"I don't want tonight to end," she said.

He lifted her chin. "It's not over yet. We're just getting started."

She smiled at him, and he hugged her. He didn't want to think beyond their lovemaking. He didn't want to dwell on his damaged career or the mess he'd made of his life.

He took her hand and led her to the bedroom. Her bed was unmade, the lace-covered pillows scattered. He dug into his pocket and removed his lighter. She stepped back while he lit the candles on her dresser. When he turned out the light, the room glowed.

"It's my turn to make you crazy," he said. His turn to give her what she'd given him.

* * *

Natalie took a moment to watch Zack undress, to remove his jeans and shoes. Shadows etched his face and danced across his body in candlelit hues. A more beautiful man didn't exist. He was everything she wanted, everything her heart desired.

He sat on the edge of the bed. "If I lie down, will you kneel over me?"

Natalie merely stared. "Over you?"

He grinned at her, a flash of teeth in the dark—a boyish look, a masculine seduction. "Over my face."

Her legs turned wobbly, and suddenly she struggled to respond. Could she be that bold?

"You liked it last time," he said.

Her skin went hot. "I know, but I wasn't sprawled over you. Making you do it."

"You won't be making me do it. I want to."

"I know, but—"

"But what?" His gaze roamed over her.

Self-conscious, she smoothed her hair, trying to draw his attention away from her nervousness. What else could she do? She was naked, and he was scrutinizing her.

"Was Halloway your first lover?" he asked.

She nodded, her pulse still lodged in her throat. "I think that's why I intrigued him so much. I lived on the streets, I ran around with teenage prostitutes, with strippers, with runaways, with kids who'd do just about anything to survive, and I was still a virgin."

"So he taught you everything you know?"

She nodded again. "That's why I'm so good at—"

She paused, searching for a polite term. "Why I'm good with my mouth. I did that to him all the time. It's what he wanted. What he liked best. But he never reciprocated."

"Selfish bastard." Zack rose to take her in his arms, and she practically melted against him.

"I'm not used to a man doing things to me," she said.

He stepped back to look at her, to graze her cheek. "I never expected you to be shy."

Her pulse fluttered. Suddenly she felt young and inexperienced, hardly the mistress she'd become.

He grabbed her waist and spun her toward the bed, and in the next instant, they tumbled onto the mattress, caressing, kissing, keeping each other close. He tasted like tobacco, like the menthol cigarettes he smoked, like male spices, like mint on a windy day.

"Let me love you," he said.

She opened her eyes, released an anxious breath. She couldn't deny him. Nor could she deny herself. Still a little shy, she moved forward. He reached for her and she kneeled over him, waiting and watching, her heart filled with hope. She wanted him to love her.

He kissed her inner thighs, nibbling her skin, working his way to her center. Then he touched her there—right there—with the tip of his tongue. Natalie feared she might die.

He grasped her hips and pulled her closer, directly against his mouth. He licked her, deep and slow, making her wetter than she already was.

Losing her inhibitions, she arched her back and rubbed against him, taking everything he offered, everything he was willing to give. He took her hand and encouraged her to caress herself, to heighten the sensation, the slick, wicked pleasure.

When her body shook, when her legs went molten, she let her knees sink into the bed. She sighed, then rocked to the rhythm, to the intimacy they shared.

The room spun in a haze of candlelight, in flames twirling around the bed. She made a breathy sound and watched Zack make love to her. Lost in the feeling, she touched his face, the way he'd touched her when she'd done this to him.

Unable to stop the pressure, Natalie climaxed against his mouth. With a soft moan, she stayed right where she was, kneeling over him, letting him taste her release.

Afterward, she slid down his body, down hard planes and sinewy muscles. Savoring his nakedness, she clung to him, dizzy and sated.

He nuzzled her cheek, and she closed her eyes and imagined keeping him forever, living the rest of her life in his arms.

Several minutes later, he asked, "You're not asleep, are you?"

She lifted her head. "Who? Me?"

He ran his hand down her spine, then tickled her rib cage. "Yes, you."

With a girlish laugh, she snuggled closer, burrowing against him. "Are you going to spend the night?"

"You bet I am. I'm not driving home later."

She leaned over him, studying his features, the raw-boned angles and dark, deep-set eyes. The candles still burned, sending flame-scented smoke into the air. Mesmerized, she smoothed his hair, taming the strands that fell onto his forehead. "Will you have breakfast with me tomorrow?"

"If you want me to." He rubbed his leg against hers, and she felt his body stir.

"More foreplay, Zack?"

"I was kind of hoping we could get to the real thing."

"Were you now?" She nipped his shoulder, and he tumbled her onto her back, making her squeal. When she looked up at him, her heart clawed her chest. How was she going to live without him? Face each day without his strength, his sardonic sense of humor, his tough-guy temper?

"Can we eat breakfast in bed?" she asked suddenly, wanting the morning after to be special. She couldn't bear to have him freeze up on her, the way he'd done last time.

"If I say yes, will you get kinky with me?"

She couldn't help but smile. Zack never remained serious for long. "I suppose you already have a position in mind."

"Hmm. Let's see." He made a show of furrowing his forehead. "Maybe you can stand on your head, and I can—"

She stabbed him with her nail, and he grinned.

"Missionary will do," he told her, as he pinned her hands above her head. "And just a little bondage."

Her pulse pounded at her throat. "You're a dangerous man."

"And you're an incredible woman." He released her wrists and lowered his head to kiss her, to treat her with gentleness, with the kind of care that made her love him even more.

When he entered her, she wrapped her legs around him, taking him deeper. He looked into her eyes and warmth streamed through her blood, like a river flowing through her veins.

Taking possession, he spanned her waist and ran his hands over her hips, shaping her curves, claiming her. She whispered his name and skimmed the muscles that rippled his stomach. Together, they made love. On a current of need, she thought. On a dream.

Two bodies melding into one.

The following morning, Zack awakened in a lazy lull. He rolled over and gazed at Natalie. She was still asleep, tucked under the blanket.

He smoothed her hair away from her face, struck by how angelic she looked. He knew she slept peacefully whenever he was near. That made him feel strong and protective, yet unbearably sad. She deserved more than he was willing to give. Halloway had used her, and, in a sense, Zack was using her, too.

"I'm sorry," he whispered. Sorry he couldn't make a permanent difference in her life, that he couldn't save both of them from their demons.

She stirred but didn't waken. Fighting his emotions, the desire to take her in his arms, he climbed out of bed and grabbed his jeans. He'd left his overnight bag in the car and needed to retrieve it. He was due for a shower. He scrubbed his hand across his jaw. And a shave.

When he walked into the living room, he spotted the clothes he and Natalie had left in the entryway. He picked up his shirt and bundled it into a ball. But he touched Natalie's nightgown with reverence. Then he remembered what he'd done to it last night. After he carried the soiled garment into her laundry room, he went outside to grab his bag.

Finally, he took a long, hot shower. He'd been tempted to ask Natalie to join him. But waking her up so she could arouse his libido seemed like something Halloway would've done, so he decided to fix her breakfast instead.

Dressed in a clean pair of jeans, he padded into the kitchen, his feet bare. He made a pot of coffee and while it brewed, he scrambled eggs and fried some fat-free baloney he found in the fridge. Natalie didn't have any ham or bacon, so he figured it wouldn't hurt to make do. He added toast and jam, and by the time he carried Natalie's plate into the bedroom, she was awake.

She gave him a sleepy smile. "I thought I smelled something cooking. That looks great."

"You said you wanted to eat breakfast in bed." He handed her the food and placed her coffee on the nightstand. She'd already tugged a T-shirt over her head and slipped on a pair of panties. Leopard print, he noticed. He suspected she had a jungle-theme bra to match. Without thinking, he leaned forward to kiss her, to say good morning, to greet her the way a husband greeted his wife.

She made a pleasured sound, and he pulled back. Being around Natalie made him miss the white-picket-fence fantasy he'd always believed in, the values his family had instilled in him.

"Where's your breakfast?" she asked.

"In the kitchen. I couldn't carry it all." He wondered if Natalie hoped to get married someday or if Halloway had destroyed that dream. He tilted his head and noticed how cozy she seemed, how comfortable in the domestic setting. "You would make somebody a really good wife."

"Really?" The plate on her lap teetered. "You think so?"

"Sure, but I'm not an expert." Uncomfortable, he shifted his stance, wishing he'd kept his mouth shut, that his emotions hadn't trapped him. "I'll be right back. I'm going to get my food."

When he returned, her expression had grown dark. "What's the matter?"

"What I did was wrong, Zack. I had no right to sleep with a married man. To be his mistress."

Balancing his plate, he sat on the edge of the bed. "Yes, it was wrong. I can't tell you how much it hurts to be cheated on. But what Halloway did to you on the day of the murder was worse. And his wife vowing to see you dead isn't any better."

"I know, but that doesn't excuse my behavior." She toyed with her fork. "Marriage is sacred, and I desecrated it."

Zack reached for his coffee. "That doesn't mean you should deprive yourself of finding the right guy someday and having a couple of kids." Because he wanted to touch her, he kept the cup in his hand, using it as a barrier. "You were great with Brice and Timmy."

She smiled. "So were you." A second later, her smile fell. "David has kids. Two teenage girls. They probably think I'm the biggest slut in the world."

Zack could see the shame in her eyes, the regret, the mistakes she couldn't undo. But he'd seen her remorse before. He knew she battled with her past. "I don't understand why Halloway's wife is laying all the blame on you. She should have divorced her husband. Told him to go to hell a long time ago."

"Ellen likes being a mobster's wife. She likes the power. She isn't about to let that go, not without a fight."

"So she's remaining loyal to Halloway, even if he's locked up? Even if she knows he's a liar and a cheat? A cold-blooded killer? They belong together. Neither of them have any morals." He sipped his coffee, then frowned. "Not that I have room to talk, considering what's going on in my life."

"Me, neither. I'm as guilty as you are."

"That's why we need to move on, Natalie." He took a rough breath, wishing he could keep her, wishing they were average people in a normal situation. "Everything's just too damn complicated between us."

"I know," she said. "But no matter what, I'll always think of you as my friend. I've never been this close to anyone before. You're the first person, man or woman, who's treated me with respect.''

Her comment only managed to make him feel worse. She was praising him for a friendship he was bound and determined to destroy.

A friendship that was even more painful than his divorce.

Twelve

On Sunday afternoon, Natalie stood in her driveway. Yesterday, she'd become the owner of a used Mustang. In a sense, this was her first car, or at least the first vehicle that hadn't been supplied by David Halloway.

She studied the ragtop and closed her hand around the keys. She wouldn't be relying on Zack to drive her to the market anymore. He wouldn't be stopping by to chauffeur her around town.

She unlocked the door and climbed behind the wheel, intending to drive to the lake, to watch boats speed across the water, to spend some time alone. But once she was on the road, she took the highway to Spokane.

To visit Zack.

Dear God. Her knuckles turned white. Would he be surprised to see her? Would he even be home?

Over an hour later, she turned onto his street and parked in front of his house. His garage was open, and she asked herself what she was trying to accomplish by coming here.

Then suddenly she knew. It was time to let him go.

She closed her eyes. Could she do it? Could she end their relationship? Free him from his emotional duty to her? She opened her eyes and released a shaky breath. What choice did she have? She couldn't bind him forever.

When she looked up, she saw that Zack had just entered the garage from his laundry room. As soon as she exited her car, he spotted her.

She stood for a moment, frozen in time. They gazed at each other and her heart went weak. He wore an old T-shirt and threadbare jeans, with a soda in his hand and a rag stuffed in his back pocket. He'd been working on his truck, she realized. Then had gone inside for a cold drink.

Finally, she took a step toward his house, and he came out of the garage. They hadn't made love since Thursday, since the night of that desperate phone call, but they both wanted to. Every time they saw each other, they struggled not to kiss, she thought. Not to lose themselves in the forbidden.

"I wasn't expecting you," he said, his voice much too rough.

"I wasn't planning on coming. It just sort of happened." The way their lovemaking had just happened, the way everything between them seemed to take on a life of its own.

He had shadows beneath his eyes, proof that he hadn't been sleeping, that their relationship plagued his nights—the way loneliness and fear devoured hers.

He extended the unopened can, offering her his drink. "Are you thirsty?"

She released the air in her lungs. "No, but thank you." She longed to kiss him, to brush his mouth with her lips, to seduce him into her arms. But that would only make her feel like the whore David had accused her of being. How many times could she stumble into bed with Zack? Sleep with a man who was still her field inspector?

He gestured to his front stoop. "Do you want to sit down?"

She nodded, and they sat across from each other on the cement step. His house was flanked by foliage, and she could smell the blooming flowers.

He flipped the top on the soda, and it made a popping sound. She watched him take a drink, saw the muscles in his neck move as he swallowed the liquid.

"I'm sorry," she said.

"For what?" He tilted his head. His hair was mussed and his shirt bore faded grease stains.

"For everything. What I've been doing to you isn't fair."

"I promised I wouldn't rush you." He placed his hand on her knee, a touch that was far from casual. "I'm not going to walk away from you until you're ready.'' He curled his fingers into her skirt, bunching the summer fabric.

Natalie knew she would never be ready. She would love him until her dying day. ''I can't keep prolonging the inevitable.''

He took his hand back. ''So it's over?''

She folded her arms across her stomach. ''You're the one who said we couldn't stay friends. That it wouldn't benefit either of us.'' She watched him, waiting for him to respond, praying that he would change his mind. That he would declare that he couldn't live without her.

He cleared his throat. ''Be sure to tell your doctor about your nightmares. Tell her what you told me.''

''I will.'' Was that his way of accepting her decision? Of letting her go?

He glanced up, shielding his eyes from the late-day sun. ''I'll turn in my resignation tomorrow.''

Still clutching her middle, she followed his gaze. Clouds floated across the sky, shape-shifting, melting like marshmallows. When she cried for him, she would cry alone. She wouldn't let him know how much it hurt. ''Are you going to move to Illinois?''

''I think so, yeah. I can't bear to stay here.''

Silence drifted between them. She would never tell him that she loved him. What point would there be? It would only cause more tension, more sadness.

He shifted his gaze to her Mustang, staring at the vehicle, his voice still rough. ''I'm surprised you chose a white car. I pictured you in red.''

Why? Because red was flashy? Because it fit her

tall, blond image? "I like white." To her, it represented purity, something that had been lacking in her life.

"So do I, but you look good in red."

"I look good in white, too." As an image of a traditional wedding gown came to mind, she pushed away the thought. This wasn't the time to dwell on girlhood hopes, on shattered dreams.

He turned toward her, and their gazes locked. She wanted to put her head on his shoulder, but that would only fuel the ache.

"Are you going to visit your Lakota family?" she asked, wondering if making peace with his heritage would help him start over.

He shook his head. "I've got enough to contend with. I couldn't handle a rejection. Not now."

"I don't think they'll reject you, Zack."

He gave her a troubled smile. "That's because you're biased."

No, she thought. She was in love.

Silent, she studied his features, the lines at the corners of his eyes, his bronzed skin, the cheekbones that boasted his ancestry. "Can't you let Wounded Knee go? Can't you put it behind you?"

"How can I do that? Do you know how significant Wounded Knee is? There's more to it than the siege my uncle was involved in." He reached for a fallen leaf, turning it over in his hand. "In 1890, three-hundred Sioux were massacred at Wounded Knee. Men, women and children. They were seeking salvation in the Ghost Dance, in a religious practice,'' he explained. ''And the army slaughtered them for it.''

''Then go there.'' She moved a little closer, nearly brushing his shoulder, nearly touching. ''Let it be part of your spirit.''

''That's a romantic concept, but it's unrealistic. I'm not going to hear my ancestors' voices. They're not going to slip into my dreams.'' He paused to finish his soda, to crush the empty can. ''I'll always be more white than Indian.''

''Your father was Sioux. You're half Sioux.''

''That doesn't make me Indian. Not in a traditional sense.''

Natalie gave up the argument. When she looked into his eyes, she saw both sides of his heritage. She saw the boy who'd been raised by his white mother, the same boy who'd never forgotten his Lakota father.

He glanced away, and her breath lodged in her throat. She was losing him. Yet there was nothing she could do about it. Nothing but keep him locked inside her heart. The way he kept his father's quilt tucked away in a cedar chest, gathering bittersweet memories.

Voices in the wind, she thought. Voices he couldn't hear.

Hours later, Zack sat across from his mother in her room at the nursing home. Dusk had long since fallen, and he could see darkness from her window.

He could scarcely breathe. The sudden emptiness in his life was almost too much to bear. He needed to talk to someone, so he'd come to see his mom, yet her befuddled state only made the hole in his heart bigger.

His mom was ignoring him. Confused, it seemed, by his gift. She frowned at the bottle of glitter nail polish. She wasn't interested in being a fairy this evening.

"Do you know who I am?" he asked.

She looked up. Still frowning, she measured him with her childlike gaze. "You're that boy who has a smash on me."

He found the strength to smile. "A crush. Not a smash."

"You brought me some paint." She placed the bottle in the palm of her hand. "It's so small. And it has strange things in it."

He decided not to explain why he'd given it to her. He doubted she would want to polish her nails. Her moods and her interests weren't easy to follow.

"You seem sad," she said, setting her rocker in motion.

"I am." He watched the bottle fall from her hand and roll onto the floor, disappearing under her dresser. "I can't stay close to the woman I care about."

Her gaze snared his. "To Juliet?"

"Yes." He was grateful that she remembered who Natalie was, or at least who she thought Natalie was. It was better than no memory at all. "I'm going to be moving away, and I won't see her anymore."

"Because she's a Capulet."

"Because I'm a deputy marshal and she's my witness. We're not allowed to be together."

"Then don't be a deputy marshal." She smoothed her robe. She was already dressed for bed, her hair brushed away from her face. "Just don't be one."

"I've already decided to do that. I'm leaving my job."

"So there." She waved her hands in a grand gesture, like a magician completing a trick. "Now you can be with her."

"It's not that simple."

"Why not?"

"I—" Suddenly he couldn't think of a logical response. Nothing came into his mind but fear.

"Do you love her?" she asked.

Did he? He closed his eyes, squeezing them tight. He hadn't considered it until now, but it was there, deep in his heart, winding barbed wire around his soul. "Yes," he finally said. "I love her."

"Then marry her."

He opened his eyes, struggled to steady his jarring pulse. Did he want to marry Natalie? To make the ultimate commitment?

Yes, he thought. Deep down, he did. He could imagine sharing his life with her. She'd become his friend, as well as his lover. He knew she would make a loyal, passionate wife. But there were complications, anxieties he couldn't deny. WITSEC discouraged witnesses from telling prospective spouses that they were in the Witness Protection Program. Secrecy was a matter of keeping witnesses safe. If a marriage faltered, a former spouse could take revenge, jeopardizing a witness's security. A spouse wasn't supposed to be told, not unless he or she was forced to enter WITSEC.

And that was Zack's fear: entering a program that had been tailored for criminals. He wasn't afraid of the danger. He was trained to deal with high-risk situations. But he didn't like the idea of living on the other side, of surviving the emotional baggage, of losing his name, his family history—everything that made him who he was.

He dragged his hand through his hair. "If I married her and her security was breached, if someone from her past recognized her, or if the mob uncovered her new name, I'd have to change my identity, too."

His mother didn't understand. She merely stared at him as if he'd grown a set of spiral-shaped horns.

Zack shook his head, rattling his thoughts. "That doesn't make sense, does it?" Loving someone meant making sacrifices, and he was afraid of giving up his name, of becoming someone new. Yet he helped other people do that very thing. "I don't even know how she feels about me. She wants to stay friends, but that isn't the same as being in love."

"Juliet loves Romeo. She died for him."

"I'm not Romeo." And he didn't want to dwell on death. Natalie was already marked for a mob hit. He knew WITSEC would keep her safe, but the danger would never go away. Nor would the Witness Protection lifestyle. "I don't know what to do. I'm confused."

"I get confused sometimes."

He glanced up. "I know you do."

"Is that why you visit me?"

"I visit you because I love you."

A frown marred her brow. She stopped the rocker and gave a heavy sigh. "You love Juliet. She's the one you should marry."

"I love you in a different way. Like a mother."

"Then you and Juliet can give me grandchildren." She set the chair in motion again. "Doris has grandchildren. All she does is brag."

Zack blew out a rough breath. Doris, another patient at the nursing home, had died two months ago. And the grandchildren she used to boast about didn't exist. "What if Juliet isn't in love with me?"

She scolded him in a soft voice, refusing to accept his insecurity. "I already told you she was."

"What if I can't cope with being her husband?" he asked, as his heart pounded a panicked rhythm to his brain. What if he couldn't handle being married to a witness?

At the stroke of midnight, Natalie's phone rang. She dashed to answer it, nearly tripping over the laundry she'd been sorting.

When Zack's voice came over the line, she sank into a chair. He sounded troubled.

"I didn't wake you, did I?" he asked.

"Me? At this hour? It's still early." Cinderella's curfew didn't apply to Natalie. She didn't own a pair of glass slippers.

"I've been driving around half the night," he said.

"Are you close by?"

"Yes."

She glanced at the heap of clothes. Was he hoping to come over? To have sex with her? To say goodbye one more time? "I can't sleep with you again, Zack." She couldn't commit emotional suicide. Not now. "It's better if we leave things as they are."

"That's what I've been saying all along. But I can't stand it. I'm going nuts."

"I can't be your mistress." Not even for one night. One long, lonely night.

"This isn't about sex."

"Then what's it about?"

"Getting married," he said.

The phone slipped from her ear. "What?"

"Can I come over?"

Her legs began to tremble. "Yes." *Oh, God.* "Yes."

He arrived in a shambles. His suit was wrinkled; his hair tousled from raking his hands through it. They stood in the middle of her living room, staring at each other. Déjà vu, she thought. How many times had they been caught in this very same moment?

Except for the marriage part.

"Tell me what's going on," she said.

He shifted his stance, then looked away. Uncomfortable. Anxious. She'd never seen him lose his cool, not like this.

"Zack?"

"I'm in love with you. Damn it." He fumbled for a cigarette, cursed his habit and tossed the unopened pack onto her coffee table. "I'm in love with a witness."

She feared she might faint. She gripped the back of a chair, nearly saw the room turn white. "Since when?"

"Since... I don't know. I just figured it out tonight. My mom asked me if I loved Juliet." He grabbed his cigarettes again. "And she thinks Juliet loves me."

Natalie's eyes turned watery. "Your mother is right. Juliet would do almost anything to keep you."

"Anything but become my mistress."

"Yes."

"I'm not looking for a mistress. I want a wife." He unwrapped the pack and jammed the cellophane into his pocket. "But I never banked on marrying someone in the program."

Her heart fell. "So this isn't a proposal?"

"I don't know what it is." He retrieved a cigarette and stuck it between his lips. "Can we go outside?"

She took a freshly washed sweater out of the laundry pile and followed him onto the patio. He flicked his lighter, cupped his hands and shielded the flame from the wind. Then he inhaled the tobacco and nicotine, dragging hard and deep.

"You should move away," she said. "You should follow through with your original plans."

He shook his head. "I can't. Don't you see? I can't leave you behind. I need you."

She blinked back her tears. No one had ever needed her before. "Then what's wrong?"

"Everything is changing. I've been in control of

keeping people safe, of helping them adjust to their new lives. And now I could become one of them." He blew a line of smoke into the night air. "If I marry you and your security is breached, I'd have to enter the program, too."

She buttoned her sweater, burrowing into it, searching for artificial warmth. "Then walk away."

"But I want to be your husband. The guy who shares your hopes and dreams, who fathers your children, who makes breakfast for you every morning. Whenever I'm not around you, I go crazy."

She swiped at her tears. "Then stay. Be with me."

"Go. Stay." His voice broke. "You're a lot of help."

"And you're my protector," she told him, exposing her heart. "Nothing can take away your strength, the qualities that make you who you are." She paused to meet his gaze. "If you were my husband, I'd always be happy. It wouldn't matter how many times my security was breached or how many times our identities were changed, you'd still be the same man I fell in love with. Your soul would be the same."

He moved toward her. "How did you get so wise?"

"I had a good teacher."

He snuffed out his cigarette and slipped his arms around her. "Who? That smart-mouth inspector of yours?"

"Yes." She put her head on his shoulder. She could feel the warmth of his body, the stone-skimming beat of his heart, the desperate way he held her.

"Will you marry me?" he asked.

She lifted her head, stepped back to look in his eyes. "Are you sure, Zack? If you still have doubts—"

"I don't. Not now. Not anymore." Suddenly he'd never been so sure of anything in his life. Being with her was the light at the end of the tunnel. He was her safety net and she was his. As long as they were husband and wife, he would survive, he would learn to adjust to the changes that came his way, to follow his heart the way she was following hers. "You're more important than my job or my identity or anything else I've been afraid of losing. We can start over together. We can build a happy future, no matter what happens."

She touched his face, and his pulse pounded at his throat. He'd never felt so alive.

He leaned forward and they all but fell into each other's embrace. He inhaled the scent of her hair, the fragrance of her skin. What could be more perfect? The moon and the stars and the woman he loved.

"Juliet," he said.

She smiled against his lips, then kissed him, long and slow and sweet. She tasted like cherry cola on a summer day, like lighthearted dreams and cozy memories.

He scooped her up and she looped her arms around his neck.

"Where are we going?" she asked.

"To bed. To cuddle," he clarified. He carried her into the house and shouldered his way into her room.

Snuggled beside each other, they leaned against her

pillows. Zack removed his jacket and tossed it on a chair. Natalie's sweater followed.

She rested her hand on his thigh. "Where are we going to live?"

"Here. Not in this house, but in Coeur D'Alene. This is where you're establishing your identity, where you plan to launch a boutique." He smoothed her hair, slipping his fingers through the feathered strands. "And you're already registered for school."

"Your other witnesses are going to miss you."

Touched by her belief in him, he smiled. He'd never talked to her about any of his other witnesses. That was a rule he hadn't broken. "WITSEC will take care of them. And as soon I put in my resignation, you'll have another inspector, too."

"I don't need anyone but you."

"Yes, you do. You'll need someone on the inside." Zack would protect her every moment he could, but the Marshal Service had the manpower. They could send a squad of deputies to her aid, ready to take down anyone who tried to hurt her.

"Are you going to open a security-consulting firm in Coeur d'Alene?" she asked.

"Or in Spokane. It's easy enough to commute." He met her gaze. He liked her girlish excitement, the questions that prodded him to plot and plan their future, to cement their lives. "I can sell my house and we can buy a place in this neighborhood, if you want. We can spend time at my cabin, too. It can be our home away from home."

"I just want to be your wife." Bright eyed, she all but sighed. "Can we have a traditional wedding?"

"A long white dress? A tuxedo? Shiny gold rings?"

"Yes." She gave him a dreamy smile. "To have and to hold from this day forward."

He pictured lifting a lace veil from her face, looking into her eyes, kissing her. "I'd like that. Maybe we can get married in the garden at the nursing home. I know that sounds a little strange, but it would be easier for my mom and I want her to be there, to be part of it."

"I think that's a perfect idea. She should be there. She should see her son get married."

"Even if she can't remember I'm her son." He thought about his mother's befuddled request for grandchildren. "How many kids do you want?"

Natalie adjusted the sheet, draping it over them, letting it flutter like a spring breeze. "At least two. That way, they'll always have each other."

"Yeah. Being an only child can get lonely." He paused to take a much-needed breath, to take their plans a step further. "Maybe I should go to the reservation and get acquainted with my father's family. After things settle down. After we're married." He turned toward her. "Will you come with me? Will you be by my side?"

She pressed her palm to his cheek. "You know I will."

They sat silently after that, immersed in each other, in the beauty of being in love, in accepting whatever fate had to offer.

She reached for him, and he knew she was inviting him to hold her, to watch over her while she slept, to keep her safe. He accepted the responsibility without question.

She closed her eyes, and he left the light on so he could look at her, so he could memorize every feature, every beautiful angle of her face.

"My Natalie," he whispered, knowing their lives, the world they would create, had just begun.

Epilogue

Natalie rode beside her husband in a rented SUV, gazing out the window at the vast South Dakota terrain. This wasn't their first trip to the Pine Ridge Reservation. During the two years they'd been married, they'd visited Zack's family on numerous occasions. His grandmother was gone, but his aunt, his father's older sister, was still alive and he had a slew of cousins. He wasn't the enemy. He was blood, and they accepted him.

She looked over at him. He reached for her hand and held it. She knew these trips made him emotional. The reservation encompassed about two-million acres, but the statistics affiliated with it weren't nearly as grand. Over sixty percent of the population lived below poverty level. The unemployment rate far exceeded the national average, and many families dwelled in overcrowded homes. Some of those homes had no electricity, no telephone and no running water.

Zack's family members fared somewhat better, as some of his cousins were fortunate enough to have steady jobs, but there were still a lot of mouths to feed. Zack did whatever he could to help them. He'd cashed in a portion of his retirement fund to improve the quality of their lives, but generosity was the Indian way. On the reservation, even the poor helped the poor. Relatives, no matter how distant, were never turned away, which accounted for the overly crowded conditions. When guests arrived at a Lakota home, food was quickly prepared and served, even if there was little to be had.

Today they were celebrating a birthday. One of Zack's third cousins was turning seven.

Silent, they traveled along an unpaved road. The sky was as blue as a calm-hearted sea, and the land was rich in tones from the earth. This was God's country, Natalie thought. God's people.

She touched her tummy, where Zack's child rested. She was three months pregnant and glowing with maternal pride. She couldn't wait for her stomach to swell, for the baby they'd created to grow.

Finally, he parked beside his aunt's house, and a group of kids swarmed the car. Zack was their big, handsome cousin.

He exited the driver's side and scooped up the birthday girl. She slipped her arms around his neck and giggled. Her eyes were dark and trusting and her hair swung down her back in a long, loose ponytail. She felt safe in Zack's arms. But who wouldn't? He was strong and protective, with a giving spirit.

"We brought you a bunch of presents." He nuzzled the young girl and ruffled the hair of a pint-size boy. "We brought all of you presents." Then he turned to look at Natalie.

She knew he was happy. For him, this was like coming home. The voices of his ancestors did exist and he heard them daily. He'd learned some Lakota words, and he was anxious to teach their child. Sometimes he talked to her tummy, telling their unborn baby stories his aunt had told him.

But most of all, he'd made peace with Wounded Knee, a place the Lakota called *Cankpe Opi*. It was part of his history, part of his pain, but it was part of his healing, as well. The Lakota were a proud people, struggling to retain their culture and traditions. And Zack was one of them.

He reached for her hand and they entered his aunt's home, with a passel of kids chattering at their heels.

Life was good, Natalie thought. She was happy, too. Her ordeal with the mob had made her stronger. She'd testified at David's trial, giving a deposition that included the things he'd done to her on the day of the murder.

She would always be monitored by WITSEC, but she and Zack lived normal, productive lives. Their future was in the Creator's hands and they thanked Him every day for bringing them together.

Natalie's nightmares had long since passed. These

days she focused on home and hearth, on growing old with the man she loved. Her husband, she thought. The father of her unborn child, the man who filled her soul with warmth, with dreams of years to come.

*   *   *   *   *

Look for Sheri WhiteFeather's next
work, a contribution to the special
DANFORTH ANTHOLOGY,
DYNASTIES: SUMMER IN SAVANNAH,
available June 2004 from Silhouette Books.

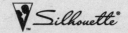

COMING NEXT MONTH

#1579 THE BOSS MAN'S FORTUNE—Kathryn Jensen
Dynasties: The Danforths
Errant heiress Katie Fortune had left home and her oppressive lifestyle behind and began anew—as secretary to Ian Danforth. The renowned playboy was a genius in the boardroom. But it was his bedroom manner that Katie couldn't stop fantasizing about....

#1580 THE LAST GOOD MAN IN TEXAS—Peggy Moreland
The Tanners of Texas
She'd come to Tanner's Crossing looking for her family. What Macy Keller found was Rory Tanner, unapologetic ladies' man. Rory agreed to help with Macy's search—to keep an eye on her. But as the sexual tension began to hum between them, it became difficult to keep his *hands* off her!

#1581 SHUT UP AND KISS ME—Sara Orwig
Stallion Pass: Texas Knights
Sexy lawyer Savannah Clay was unlike any woman he'd ever known. Mike Remington hadn't believed she'd take him up on his marriage proposal—if only for the sake of the baby he'd inherited. Falling into bed with the feisty blonde was inevitable; it was falling in love that Mike was worried about....

#1582 REDWOLF'S WOMAN—Laura Wright
When Ava Thompson had left Paradise, Texas, four years ago, she'd carried with her a little secret. But her daughter was not so little anymore. Unsuspecting dad Jared Redwolf was blindsided by the truth—and shaken by the power Ava had over him still. Could the passion they shared see them through?

#1583 STORM OF SEDUCTION—Cindy Gerard
Tonya Griffin was a photographer of the highest repute...and Web Tyler wanted her work to grace the pages of his new magazine. But Web also had other plans for the earthy beauty...and they didn't involve work, but the most sensual pleasures.

#1584 AT ANY PRICE—Margaret Allison
Kate Devonworth had a little problem. Her small-town paper needed a big-time loan, and her childhood crush turned wealthy investor Jack Reilly was just the man to help. Kate resolved to keep things between them strictly business...until she saw the look in his eyes. A look that matched the desire inside her....

SDCNM0404